"I'm not sure I believe you when you said you didn't feel anything earlier today. When we kissed in front of the cameras."

Logan's voice was low, resonating throughout her body. It wasn't just the kiss that made her feel something. Everything about him made her feel, and that was a terrifying feeling. Leaving herself open to him eventually led to hurt. Always.

A heavy sigh escaped her lungs. "It was a kiss. It didn't change my world," she lied.

Logan reared back his head and brought their dance to a stop. "I don't believe you."

"It was hours ago. I hardly even remember It."

"Then let me refresh your memory."

He clutched her neck and lowered his lips to hers. His mouth drifted to her cheek, his stubble scratching her nose, then he traveled to her jaw and kissed her neck. She kept her eyes closed, luxuriating in every heavenly press of his lips, not wanting it to end.

"Tell me you don't feel anything," he whispered into her ear.

"I don't feel anything." The truth was that she was feeling everything right now. Her entire body was so alert she could probably stay awake for the next twenty-four hours.

"You said it yourself earlier today. You're a terrible liar."

Dear Reader,

Thanks for picking up a copy of my latest for Harlequin Desire, *The Best Man's Baby*. If you read *That Night with the CEO*, you will recognize my heroine, Julia Keys. She was Adam Langford's fake girlfriend! After I wrote that first book, my editor said, "I hope Julia gets her own book." Funny, but I had been thinking the same thing.

In this story, Julia and her high school sweetheart, Logan Brandt, are fighting history—misunderstandings, hurt feelings and mistakes. It was a lot of baggage for my poor characters to handle. I wanted to focus on what could be fresh and new about their love, and that comes in the form of Julia's pregnancy. There are many unknowns for Julia and Logan, and they both have to see that's part of what makes their love special. Facing an uncertain future, they must work hard to find their happily-ever-after.

I set this book in the beautiful seaside town of Wilmington, NC. I live in North Carolina and love to visit our stunning beaches whenever possible. I hope you enjoy this romantic and picturesque Southern escape, all set against the backdrop of the inevitable, comical fiascos that come with being the maid of honor and best man.

If you enjoy this book, please drop me a line at karen@karenbooth.net. I love to hear from readers!

Karen

KAREN BOOTH

—

THE BEST MAN'S BABY

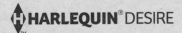

Recycling programs
for this product may
not exist in your area.

ISBN-13: 978-0-373-83823-3

The Best Man's Baby

Copyright © 2017 by Karen Booth

Printed in U.S.A.

Karen Booth is a Midwestern girl transplanted in the South, raised on '80s music, Judy Blume and the films of John Hughes. She writes sexy, big-city love stories. When she takes a break from the art of romance, she's teaching her kids about good music, honing her Southern cooking skills or sweet-talking her husband into whipping up a batch of cocktails. Find out more about Karen at karenbooth.net.

Books by Karen Booth

Harlequin Desire

That Night with the CEO
Pregnant by the Rival CEO
The CEO Daddy Next Door
The Best Man's Baby

Visit her Author Profile page at Harlequin.com, or karenbooth.net, for more titles.

For Bryony Evens, my sweet and lovely friend.
May the handsome guy in the flower shop
always flirt with you.

One

Julia Keys ducked out of the cab in front of her childhood home amid a hailstorm of camera flashes and shouts from reporters.

Where's Derek, Julia? Is he flying in from LA for your sister's wedding?

Is it true you and Derek are shopping for a house together?

Any chance you and Derek will tie the knot?

Ludicrous questions, and yet they kept coming. She wouldn't date Derek, her current costar, if her life depended on it. The idea made her queasier than her first trimester morning sickness, and that was saying a lot.

Dodging reporters and lugging a week's worth of designer clothes in a roller bag, she marched up the

walk, past the rhododendron that had been in full
bloom at the beginning of summer, the last time she'd
been back in Wilmington. That was also the last time
Logan Brandt had stomped on her heart. The very last
time. Or at least that was the plan.

Her father raced down the stairs of the wraparound
porch and folded her into his arms. "Y'all need to
learn some manners," he yelled to the media militia
assembled at the curb.

At least the local press had enough respect to stay
off private property. The same could not be said for
the paparazzi in a big city like New York or Los An-
geles. A film career spanning nearly a decade had left
Julia a reluctant pro. Judging by the frantic phone call
from her publicist that morning, when the story of her
nonexistent romance first broke, the press would be
arriving in waves over the next several hours.

"Sorry about that, Daddy. Don't talk to them.
They'll go away if we don't say anything." She pressed
a kiss to her father's clean-shaven face. It was framed
by thick, chocolate-brown hair—the same color as
Julia's, except his had gone salt-and-pepper at the temples. The few wrinkles he had showed deep concern.
Of course he was worried—one daughter was getting married, and the other, according to the strangers still yammering at them, had questionable taste
in men. When her real predicament—the one that
would make her father a granddad—finally came to
light, she could only hope he'd stay as relatively calm
as he was now.

Her father ushered her inside, which was only

about ten degrees cooler than the eighty-degree day. She knew better than to ask her dad to adjust the thermostat. As far as he was concerned, it was September, and therefore autumn, which meant air-conditioning was no longer needed. Never mind that summer in coastal North Carolina could stretch on until Halloween.

Her mother strolled into the living room wearing a pink sleeveless blouse and white capri pants, auburn hair back in a ponytail, pearls completing the look, as always. She wiped her hands with a checkered kitchen towel. Julia's younger sister, Tracy, brought up the rear. Spitting image of their mother and the bride-to-be, Tracy was a fresh-faced vision in a turquoise sundress, staring down Julia as if she were evil incarnate. Julia was now liking her chances with the school of piranha masquerading as the media outside.

Mom offered a hug and a kiss. "It's good to see you, hon. I feel so spoiled having you home for the second time in three months."

Three months. Just enough time to get pregnant. "The high school reunion was one thing. It's not every day my baby sister gets married." Julia went in for a hug from her sister.

Tracy was having none of that, planting her hands on her hips. "How long are we going to pretend that Jules isn't ruining my wedding? If y'all are going to stand around and chitchat like nothing is wrong, I'm asking Carter to fix me a stiff drink."

It physically hurt to know that her arrival didn't warrant a hug, but Julia couldn't blame her sister. If the roles had been reversed, she'd be mad as a hornet about the frenzy in the front yard. "I'm sorry about the mess outside, but it's all a stupid lie. The press has been hinting at something between Derek and me since before we even started filming. Trust me, I'm not involved with him."

"I saw the photos. You're practically kissing him." Her mother's sweet drawl teetered on *practically*. "Are you denying it because you're not proud of the way he's behaved? They said he's been arrested for public intoxication seven times. Why would you want to be with a man like that?"

Julia shook her head, sweat already beading up on her skin. If the press could sell this contrivance of a story to her own mother, they could convince anyone. "Mom. Listen to me." She grasped her shoulders. "I swear there's nothing going on with Derek. Yes, it looks like a kiss. We were rehearsing a scene. I have zero interest in him. And he has no interest in me." *And he has the world's worst breath.*

"Then go outside and tell those buzzards precisely that." Julia's father teased back the drapes, peering outside. "We spent an awful lot of money on this wedding. I'm not about to see it ruined."

If only her father knew the lengths to which Julia was already going to *not* ruin her sister's wedding— namely keeping a pregnancy under her hat, which was absolutely killing her. Why couldn't things be normal? Just once? If her life were normal, she'd walk into this room and tell her parents she was pregnant. Her mother would probably burst with excitement, then sport the start of a nine-month-long smile and ask a million questions. Her father would sidle up to Julia's loving, handsome husband and congratulate him with a firm handshake and a clap on the back. But of course, things couldn't be normal. No husband had materialized in Julia's twenty-nine years on earth, and that was of little consequence compared to not knowing whether her ex or Logan Brandt was the baby's father. Oops.

"You have to trust me," Julia said. "If we say anything, they'll just ask more questions. We should ignore them and focus on Tracy." *Please. Anything so I can stop fixating on wanting to blurt out that I have a tiny top-secret bundle of joy in my belly.*

Tracy snorted and shook her head. "Focus on me." Plopping down on the end of the couch, she broadcast her anger by aggressively flipping through a bridal magazine. "That's rich coming from you right now." Tracy had never been much for mincing words. Why start now?

Their father sat in his wingback chair. "Jules, I know you think you know what you're doing, but I've had my own experience with the media." Julia's father had been a state senator for two decades. Twenty-one squeaky-clean, scandal-free years. "If they've fabricated this much, they'll speculate until the cows come home. Who knows what they'll come up with next."

A heavy sigh came from her mother. "I can't even think about this anymore. I need to keep myself busy in the kitchen. Maybe open a bottle of chardonnay."

"See? Now your mother is upset. I didn't pay all this money for a scandal and an unhappy wife."

"Is that all you care about?" Tracy blurted. "The money? What people will say?"

"I have a reelection campaign to run next year. My family should be an asset, not a political liability."

Tracy tossed the magazine aside. "I swear to God, it's like I'm not even getting married. Julia and money and Dad's job are obviously far more important."

"We've never had a family scandal before, Trace. I intend to keep it that way."

Family scandal. If only they knew. Julia took a deep breath, but it made her head swim. A smooth start to Tracy's wedding was out the window, and it was all her fault. The guilt of that alone was overwhelming. Tracy had played second fiddle in the Keys family for the last decade, simply because of Julia's success. People were always making a fuss, as much as Julia tried to deflect. It was time for her sister to have center stage. Then Julia could avoid the family microscope and find the perfect time to break the baby news, only after the wedding was over and the happy couple was on a cruise ship to the Bahamas.

Tracy's fiancé, Carter, came downstairs. "Logan just pulled up."

Logan. There was that to deal with as well. Her stomach sank, adding an entirely new and unpleasant aspect to pregnancy queasiness. His hundred-watt smile painfully flashed in her memory. Then came the visions from their last time together. They'd spent nearly the entire weekend in bed. His bare chest, naked shoulders…and other glorious stretches of his tawny brown skin were all that wanted to cycle through her mind. *Damn pregnancy hormones.* Her pulse raced, stirring emotion—anger over the way Logan had ended things after the reunion, frustration over once again being the girl who never managed to do anything the right way. In between all of that was a churning sea of uncertainty. And some churning of her stomach as well. She was going to be a mom. And Logan might be the father. Or he might not. Either way, she had no choice other than to tell him, deal with his reaction and move on. There was nothing more than moving on between them, and that was to be done as two separate parties. Logan had seen to that.

But first she had to find the right time to tell him. Maybe she'd take the approach her mother did when she had potentially upsetting news to break to her father—she'd tell him while he was driving. A man could only freak out so much with two hands on the wheel.

Parked on the narrow tree-lined street, several houses down from the grand Victorian the Keys family had lived in since he could remember, Logan Brandt bided his time in his rental car. Sunglasses on, flipping the keys on his finger, he studied the reporters milling about, consulting their phones. Waiting.

"What a mess," he mumbled. The buzz of activity was normal when it came to Julia. Even if she'd never become a box office hit or had her stunning face land on the cover of countless magazines, drama still would've found her. As to the cause, Logan was so tired of this scenario he could hardly see straight. Julia was once again romantically entangled with a disastrous guy. One of her projects, no doubt, as he referred to them.

His phone rang. Carter, the groom-to-be, his best friend from high school. "Hey," Logan answered. "I'm just now getting to the house."

"Liar. You're sitting in your rental car because you don't want to deal with Hurricane Julia."

"How'd you know it was me?"

"Nobody in Wilmington drives a car that expensive. Well, nobody but you."

Logan snickered. He did have an appetite for nice cars, especially if they were fast, and if anyone knew him well, it was Carter. He and Logan had met freshman year of high school at baseball tryouts. Logan landed a spot on varsity, a harbinger of things to come—full scholarship to UCLA, eight years as a major league pitcher. Record-breaking seasons. Record-breaking salaries. Then a World Series, a loss, and a career-ending injury. His trajectory had never suggested it'd all be over by the time he was thirty.

Julia was a loss of another kind, although it dogged him in much the same way. His high school sweetheart, the woman who understood him better than most, and yet she'd hurt and disappointed him countless times. He must be a glutton for punishment, because he was still wrestling with his need for Julia.

"You have to come inside and talk to Julia about getting rid of the press. Tracy is freaking out," Carter pleaded.

"I doubt she's going to listen to a thing I say after what happened after the reunion."

Julia and Logan saw each other every year at their high school reunion. The meeting had several time-honored traditions that only they were a part of. First came the downing of a cocktail, followed by merciless flirting—laughing, innocent touches, pointed glances, the flipping of hair from Julia. After the second drink came a spirited round of one-upmanship, including desperate attempts to convince the other how "happy" they were. Once full tipsiness was achieved, the painful stroll down memory lane could commence, usually ending with a heated make-out session. In those instances, one of them was to cut it short before things went too far. It was customary for the other person to stomp on the brakes the following year.

The last reunion had veered off course. They'd both walked in wounded—Logan hated his new career as a network commentator covering the sport he missed terribly, while Julia had just been offered a role playing a much older woman. She'd also made mention of having been dumped by another boyfriend, but Logan had tried to ignore that part. They'd needed each other that balmy June night, and that translated into two unforgettable days in bed, making love, laughing and talking for hours.

Unfortunately, Logan had been shaken back to

reality when he got to the airport at the end of their weekend and saw a tabloid story saying there was romance brewing with her next costar—the hapless movie star named Derek. True or not, it was too powerful a reminder that Julia wasn't capable of settling down. She was too busy trying to save the world, too drawn to an endless string of loser guys. Logan refused to be one of her losers. He'd had no choice but to end things before she hurt him again.

"Sorry you had to find out about her new boyfriend like this," Carter said. "It's gotta be tough."

"I'm fine. I'd already seen the papers. I knew all about it." *Just like last time. And every other time.*

"Will you please get in here so I can offer you a beer and not feel guilty about having one myself at four in the afternoon?"

"I'll be right there."

Logan did his duty as Carter's best man, strolling down the aged sidewalk to the Keyses' house. The reporters yelled after him—mostly requests to get Julia to come outside, although there was one question about life as an athlete-turned-sports commentator. Logan didn't reply; he just waved. He wasn't about to chime in if they asked about Julia and her new boyfriend.

Mrs. Keys opened the door, welcoming him with a smile and a hug. "Logan Brandt. If my eyes don't deceive me. I hope you and Julia can play nicely today. We have enough drama for a lifetime."

Logan nodded, stepping inside and keeping an eye

peeled for Julia. "Don't you worry about us." *I'll do it for you*.

Carter waved on his way into the kitchen. "Two beers, coming up."

Tracy rose from the couch, but grabbed Logan's arms rather than taking the hug he offered. Her eyes were ringed in pink. "Will you talk to her? You might be the only person she'll listen to about getting the press to go away."

"I don't know that I have any sway with…" Her name was poised on his lips when Julia waltzed in from the kitchen. Midstride, she froze. He couldn't move, either. Their eyes locked, and he felt as though he was up to his knees in a concrete block of memories, the most recent ones the strongest—watching her sleep in the early morning as his hand followed the contour of her lower back and a smile broke across her face. When Julia was happy, the world was a beautiful place, and she gave in to it, heart and soul.

For an incoherent instant, he wished he could take back the message he'd left for her. The one that ended everything. Her pull on him registered square in the center of his chest—a tightening that said two opposing things: he couldn't live without her, but he had to stick to his guns or he'd end up romantic roadkill. "Jules."

"Logan." Julia didn't come closer, which was a good thing, albeit disappointing. She crossed her arms, building a fortress around herself. Still, her vanilla scent found his nose and warmed him from head to toe.

"How are you?" he asked. If ever there was a loaded question, that was it. Stress radiated off her, but she was as stunning as ever. Her silky chestnut hair fell about her face in waves, effortlessly sexy. His hands twitched with the memory of what it was like to have his fingers buried in it. Her peachy skin had a summer glow he couldn't place—she usually avoided the sun. It suited her. Perfectly.

"I'm fine. I'm ready to start talking about the wedding and stop talking about me," she said.

I bet.

"That's a wonderful idea," Mrs. Keys said. "I have a special treat for Carter in the kitchen, and then we'll get started. Trace, why don't we go over the schedule and you can fill us all in on the jobs we need to do."

Tracy pulled out a binder and perched on the middle cushion of the couch. Carter handed Logan a bottle of pale ale and took a seat next to his bride-to-be, putting his arm around her and kissing her temple. Logan had given Carter plenty to envy over the years, but when it came to this, Carter had him beat. Aside from a temporary breakup, Carter and Tracy's love story was uncomplicated and sweet. Logan would've done anything to have that.

Mrs. Keys triumphantly presented a platter of her world-famous deviled eggs to her future son-in-law.

Carter lunged for one the instant they were on the coffee table. "Oh, man. Thank you. I love these things." He popped it into his mouth and moaned in ecstasy.

Julia made a wretched sound and pursed her lips, turning away.

"You okay?" Logan asked as Mrs. Keys took the remaining spot on the couch, next to Tracy.

Julia clamped her eyes shut and nodded. "Bad experience with deviled eggs on set a few weeks ago. I'm fine."

"Oh, honey. I didn't know," Mrs. Keys said, as her husband grabbed several of the offending eggs. "I can put them away if you like."

Julia shook her head. "Don't worry about me. I know how much everyone loves them."

Mr. Keys sat in his chair, leaving the love seat for Julia and Logan. Once again, their gazes connected, and he had to fight to make sense of what his body was saying to him. The problem was, whenever she was in a foul mood, he had a deep longing to kiss her out of it. He was practically wired to do it.

Logan offered her a seat. "Please. Ladies first."

Julia rolled her eyes. "Such a gentleman."

"I'm just being polite."

"It's a little late for polite."

"No fighting," Tracy barked. "Julia, I swear to God, you're going to kill me. I need the maid of honor and best man to get along. The reporters are bad enough. Not that you don't have the ability to make them go away."

Julia sat, snugging herself up against the arm of the love seat, preemptively distancing herself from him. "I can only say it so many times. The story is fake. I know you all think I have the world's worst taste in men, but don't worry. I did manage to avoid this one. And if we just ignore the press, they'll leave."

Relief washed over him, followed by surprise. No romance with Derek? Really? "Julia's probably right. They'll get bored if you don't talk to them." Feeling considerably more at ease, Logan joined Julia on the love seat. "We're getting along just fine. No fighting."

Tracy's eyes darted back and forth between them. She seemed unconvinced, but returned her focus to her binder. "Give me a minute to figure out what I want everyone to do. Mom, can you look at this?"

Mrs. Keys slid closer to her daughter and the two became immersed in conversation. That left Carter and Mr. Keys to feast on deviled eggs.

Logan was still computing the revelation about Julia's costar. If the story was fake, had it always been? "So, no love connection with Derek, huh?" he asked under his breath.

"No."

"Never?"

"No, Logan. Not ever," she snipped. "After that lovely message you left for me, I'm surprised you care."

Ouch. "I never want to see you with the wrong guy, Jules."

"Okay, everybody. Listen up." Tracy straightened in her seat and started rattling off orders about the florist and picking up wedding bands, the baker and final dress fittings, like a four-star general about to lead them into battle. That left no time for Logan to continue his conversation with Julia, although he wanted to. At least to smooth things over.

Julia was scribbling notes as fast as Tracy could talk. "Got it. I'm on florist and cake duty. Don't worry. I'll take care of it. The only hitch is that I didn't rent a car." She cleared her throat. "Logan, maybe you can drive me."

"You're at the same hotel. It only makes sense," Mrs. Keys chimed in.

True. It *did* make sense, but he couldn't escape the feeling that Julia had ulterior motives. Something in her voice told him that she did. Whatever her plan, hopefully it didn't include ripping his head off and sticking it on a stake in the front yard as payback for the post-reunion breakup. "Of course. Whatever Tracy and Carter need us to do to help make this the perfect wedding."

Two

Julia was sure there was no sound more unhinging than that of reporters politely, but incessantly, rapping on the windows of Logan's rental car, raising their voices as he tried to pull away.

"These people are ridiculous. Somebody's going to get hurt." Logan inched the car out of his parking space. The second he had a clear path, he gunned it.

Julia jerked back in her seat. Her stomach lurched along with it. "Logan. Cool it." She whipped around to look behind them. The reporters were climbing into their cars. "They're following us. Of course."

Logan watched via the rearview window. "We have to get out of here. Now."

He took a sharp turn and ducked down a side street. He knew the shortcuts like the back of his hand. They both did. They'd both learned to drive on these streets. The house Logan grew up in was only seven or eight blocks away.

Logan was intensely focused, eyes darting between the mirror and the road. He ran his hand over his close-cut ebony hair. Being so near him, it was hard not to fixate on what his stubble felt like against her cheek when he kissed her. Or the way his warm and manly smell, citrusy and clean, begged her to curl up in his arms. Everything about being around him again made her chest ache. Things were so much simpler three months ago, for that brief forty-eight hours when she could kiss him and lose herself in him without reservation. Before he ended it forever.

His hands gripped the steering wheel. With the sleeves of his deep blue dress shirt rolled to his elbows, she couldn't have ignored the flex of his solid forearms if she'd wanted to. His arms could make her feel as if she were made of feathers—light as air. Ready to be taken anywhere he wished to have her.

Logan cut over again, navigating the city grid. All while inducing an acute case of nausea.

Julia crossed her arms at her waist. Maybe she'd be too busy barfing to worry about telling Logan about the baby. "Can you take it easy? I'm feeling carsick."

"First the deviled eggs, now this? You're the girl who wanted to eat corn dogs and go on every upside-down ride imaginable at the state fair. Twice."

Logan had thrown down the gauntlet, only he didn't know it. Logan was a smart guy. She could only keep her secret from him for so long. As soon as she turned down a cocktail this weekend, he'd know something was up. His eyes were trained on the road. Time to put her mother's theory to the test.

"I need to know if you can keep a secret." She rummaged through her purse. It was better if they were both busy doing something that precluded a lot of eye contact.

"About what?"

"I can't tell you or you'll know the secret."

He shook his head, taking a left onto the main road to the hotel. "Fine. As long as it doesn't involve a murder, I can keep a secret." He stopped at a yellow light. Normally, Logan would've gunned it through the intersection, but there was a police car parked at the corner.

Why had her mother never briefed her on the protocol for stoplights? This was *not* the way this was supposed to go. Her heart raced, but the secret was going to suffocate her if she didn't tell him. She had to tell him. At least the first part. Then she'd reevaluate. "I'm pregnant."

The light turned green, but he didn't go. "You're what?"

Julia pointed ahead. "It's green."

"Oh." Logan had them again under way. "You're pregnant?"

"I am." She choked back her breath, unable to come out with the part that came next. *And you might be the father.*

"I take it nobody knows? Your family didn't say a thing about it."

"Nobody knows. I've only known for about three weeks and I didn't want to overshadow Tracy."

"You have to tell your family, Jules. They won't be happy you kept this from them."

Julia swallowed hard. *And how does the maybe-father feel about me keeping the secret?* "You saw how Tracy is. She's a wreck already. It wouldn't be fair."

Julia caught sight of the hotel. They'd be there any minute. That was bringing up a whole new set of feelings. If only her mother hadn't turned her old bedroom into an office. If only there was another good hotel close to home. If only she and Logan hadn't slept together the last time she was here. Then she wouldn't be suffering from vivid flashes of hot, bittersweet memories—his welcoming pecan-brown eyes, smoldering, telling her every sexy thing he wanted to do to her, all without a single word leaving his tempting lips. He was a man of action in the bedroom, not big for talk, but when he did speak, it was usually a doozy. *You're so damn sexy, Jules. You make me want to lock the door and throw away the key.*

He'd done such a number on her. She'd been stupidly hopeful when she was last here, foolish enough to think that finally she and Logan had gotten their act straight. Then hours after they parted, he left his message. *We'll never work. Let's just admit it. Once and for all.*

And of course, if they hadn't slept together, there was a very good chance she wouldn't be in the business of keeping secrets at all. She cupped her belly with her hand. However difficult, she wanted this. She wouldn't regret her time with Logan, however painfully it had ended, if it had brought her this baby. Her baby wasn't the problem.

Logan turned into the hotel drive. "I don't know why I bothered to try to outrun anybody. The bastards are already here." He pointed to a handful of news vans in the parking lot out front.

"There are only so many hotels between here and Wrightsville Beach. It wasn't going to take them long to figure out where we were."

They pulled up to the valet stand, reporters waiting, but no attendant in sight. Logan grabbed her arm. "Hold on one second. Let me come around to your side of the car. I don't want you out there on your own. You know what these guys are like, and we're on public property now. It's not like it was at your parents' house."

"I can handle myself."

"Look, Jules. Just cut a guy some slack and let me have my macho moment, okay?"

She cracked a smile. At least chivalry wasn't dead. "I owned up to it, didn't I?"

"Yes. You did." She folded her hands in her lap to wait.

Logan climbed out of the car. The reporters shouted his name, swarming him like bees. He was at her door in a flash. "Take two steps back, everybody, and let Ms. Keys out of the car."

She put on her sunglasses and opened her door. At this point, nearly a dozen people with cameras and microphones had them surrounded. She hated this more than pretty much anything.

Julia, where's Derek?

Are you having an affair with Mr. Brandt?

The valet pushed his way through the crowd. "Oh. Wow. Mr. Brandt. Ms. Keys. I'm so sorry I wasn't out here when you pulled up."

Logan surrendered his keys and a ten. "If you could have our bags brought in, that would be great."

"You got it, Mr. Brandt. I'm a huge fan. A huge fan."

Logan smiled wide. He was always gracious with his fans. "I'll be sure to sign something for you before I check out." He held back the press with one arm while he put the other around Julia.

This probably wasn't the right message to send, not with the reporters here, but she liked feeling protected by Logan.

"Are you two a couple?" someone asked. If only they knew the extent to which they were *not* a couple, even if he could be the father of her unborn child.

Logan picked up their pace as they neared the door. Still, the throng crushed in on them. "Everybody, back off." His voice boomed above the incessant chatter. He swiped off his sunglasses and straightened, employing all six feet and several more inches of him as intimidation. His audience actually shut up for a moment. Hard to believe. "One step inside and I won't bother with hotel management. I'll call the police. Leave her alone and find some other story to chase." He took her hand, and they escaped through the revolving doors.

"Are you okay?" Logan asked, not letting go of her as they made their way through the lobby.

His touch sent tingles throughout her entire body—unrequited, one-way tingles that served no purpose other than to frustrate her. "Yes. I'm fine." She stepped up to the front desk. "Checking in. The reservation is under Brady."

"Marcia?" Logan chuckled.

"Jan Brady. I'm no Marcia," she mumbled under her breath.

The front desk clerk, who looked familiar, smiled and winked, seeming to enjoy the idea of being in on the joke of a celebrity using a false name. "But, Mr. Brandt. I see you have a reservation with us as well." Confusion washed over his face as he glanced back and forth between them.

It was then that Julia recognized the man—he'd been working the front desk when she and Logan had had their tryst. They'd ended up staying in Logan's room that time. Julia hadn't bothered to check in before the reunion, and by the time they'd arrived at the hotel, they were about to tear off each other's clothes in the lobby. Two rooms had seemed laughable.

But not anymore.

Room keys in hand, Logan and Julia filed into the elevator. An elderly couple had joined them. No one said a thing, and the quiet gave Logan's mind plenty of space to roam. Too much space. *She's pregnant?*

And it's a secret? Who in the hell is the dad? He glanced over at her. *No baby bump yet. She's known for a few weeks. She can't be very far along. Wait a minute...* How far along was she? Could he? No. Not that. But wait. Could he be? The dad?

The elevator came to a stop. Logan held the door to afford the other passengers some time. He caught the uncertainty in Julia's eyes. There was more weighing on her. He could see it, and he had to know it all, even if it might hurt. They made it to the top floor— as Logan remembered it, the only floor with suites. Judging by their room numbers, they'd be across the hall from each other.

"We should talk some more," Julia said when they'd arrived at their doors. Her voice was ragged at the edges, an apt reflection of her nerves. Considering the pressure from the reporters, her family and having to keep her secret, she had to be exhausted.

"Yes. We should. I want to hear more about your, um, situation." He felt idiotic the minute he'd worded it that way, but at least he'd kept his promise to not say anything.

"I need food, too. I'm really hungry."

"Even after being carsick?"

"Yes. It's one of the weird things about...it. I feel queasy, but I'd give my right arm for fried chicken and a peach pie. The whole pie."

He was still getting used to the idea of Julia being pregnant. Talking about it wasn't helping. It was only making it more bizarre. "With the vultures outside, we probably shouldn't leave the hotel until we need to."

"Can we order room service and talk after I have a chance to change?"

The bellman came strolling down the hall with their two roller bags.

"Looks like your change of clothes is right on time. My room? A half hour?"

"Perfect."

Logan brought his suitcase inside and ordered food—grilled pork for himself, and with no fried chicken on the menu, he chose a steak for Julia, medium rare. Just the way she liked it, and she never turned down a steak. He then unpacked his suit for the rehearsal dinner Friday night, as well as the rest of his clothes, and changed into jeans and a T-shirt. He might as well get comfortable for whatever it was that Julia was going to spring on him tonight. One thing was for sure. She had a talent for catching him off guard.

Room service was wheeling in the cart when Julia came out of her room. "Sorry I'm a little late. I nodded off for a few minutes."

She *was* tired—enough to nod off. That was so unlike Julia, he could hardly wrap his brain around it. She never slowed down. There was always something brewing, always something to do, someone new to meet, some new adventure on which to embark. So this was her new adventure. A baby.

A sweet smile that was tinged with melancholy crossed her face as she stepped inside. It struck him as she padded past, leaving her soft and sensuous smell in her wake—she seemed smaller. Was it because she was as out on a limb as a person could be, all while trying to hide? Although she rarely allowed herself to be vulnerable, Julia was a very open person. Keeping this secret from her family must've been one of the most difficult things she'd ever decided she had to do.

She'd changed into a loose-fitting pink top and a pair of black yoga pants. Julia could work a fancy designer dress like nobody's business, but he really preferred her like this—relaxed. And he had to admire the rear view as he trailed behind her. "We can sit on the sofa and eat."

They started in on dinner, Julia confirming her claim that she was starving. She'd always been an enthusiastic eater, even when she was skinny as a rail in high school, but this was an impressive showing. "I've been craving red meat, too. So thank you. This is perfect."

He smiled and nodded, not really tasting his meal, still getting accustomed to the notion of the pregnancy. He'd already psyched himself up for her to tell him who the dad was, although he dreaded the answer—some hotshot CEO, a power-hungry producer or one of her toothy costars. And then there was the voice in his head asking if he might be part of the equation.

The moment was still fresh in his mind—back in his room after the reunion, peeling away her dress, drinking in the vision of her curves, it all hitting him in an avalanche—he'd waited for a very long time to be with her again. The way she moved told him that she was far more comfortable with her body than she'd ever been in high school. As she unbuckled his belt and kissed him softly, she'd said they wouldn't need a condom. She was on the pill. She'd also quipped, "When I remember to take it." Then his pants had slumped to the floor and further clarification of birth control was the last thing on his mind. That night alone they could have conceived a baby many times over, and it had been only the start of their weekend together.

"So. Pregnant. That's big. Really big." Why he suddenly had so little vocabulary was beyond him. He only knew that his palms were starting to get clammy.

"I know. It is." She gathered her napkin and placed it on the table. "I was surprised, to say the least."

"So this wasn't planned."

"No. It wasn't."

"How far along are you?"

"Three months."

Just say it. "And how is the dad feeling about all of this?"

She twisted her lips and turned to look at him with her wide brown eyes. He'd never seen them so unsure. "I don't know, exactly. The truth is that I'm not completely certain who the father is."

His heart was thundering in his chest. He knew she had men falling at her feet, but was it really this extreme? "Oh."

"It's either my ex, the guy who dumped me right before the reunion, or...it's you."

His heart came to a complete stop. In fact, the only thing that gave him any indication the earth was still spinning was the bat of Julia's dark lashes. He sat forward and rested his elbows on his knees, nodding. Thinking. Processing. Once again, she'd surprised the hell out of him. He'd prepared for either answer. Not *both. I might be the dad? Or I might not?* He couldn't live long without knowing for sure. He sat back up. "We have to have a paternity test. Right away."

"I knew you were going to say that, but I don't really see the point. It's not going to change anything."

"It'll change a lot for me." His brain hurt from the suggestion that they not find out who the father was.

"It doesn't matter. Either way, I'm pregnant by a man who chooses not to be with me. Do you have any idea how terrible that feels? I need to focus on the good, for my own sake. I'm choosing to focus on the baby."

Logan still couldn't believe what she was saying. "I'm going to go insane sitting around for the next six months wondering whether or not I'm about to be a dad."

"I'm sorry, but that's just too bad. It's not going to change the fact that we aren't together. We'll have to wait until the baby arrives and then we'll know. It should be fairly obvious once the baby is born. I doubt we'll need a paternity test."

Ah. I see. "So the other guy isn't black?"

"He isn't."

Well, that certainly made that aspect of things con-
venient. But still the logistics made no sense. Was
he supposed to sit in a waiting room with her ex and
hope like hell that the baby came out with a skin tone
closest to his own?

"I've thought about it, and the most sensible thing
is to wait until then and you can decide how involved
you want to be. We'll have to negotiate all of that. I'm
hoping I can count on you to be sensible and flexible.
I don't want to bring in lawyers," Julia said.

His head pounded. She was discussing this as if
they were two multinational corporations preparing
to merge. "What did the other guy have to say about
all of this?" He winced at the thought of her having
this conversation with any other man, even when he
had no claim on her.

"He's out. Like all the way out. He wants nothing
to do with me. He was pretty sure I made up the baby
so I could get him back."

A low grumble left Logan's throat. What kind of
scum would think a woman like Julia would make
up a baby to get him back? And how did she end up
with a guy like that? "He's out? What does that even
mean? You get a woman pregnant, you accept responsibility. That's the first chapter of the book called *How
to Be a Real Man*."

A tear rolled down her cheek. She wrapped her
arms around herself and settled back against the
couch. "Apparently he doesn't agree."

Logan had to fight back his rage. He sucked in a

deep breath. If the baby was his, he'd take responsibility. "If it's mine, we have to get married."

A dismissive puff of air left her lips. "This is not the time for jokes."

"It's no joke. We're getting married if the baby is mine. You grew up with both parents. I…" His voice cracked, thinking about his father. "I grew up with both parents until we lost my dad. A kid needs both parents. I won't be able to live with it any other way."

"I'm not getting married to you. That's not happening."

"Yes. You are. Unlike this other guy you were with, I'm a man and I accept my responsibilities. We have to get married if the baby is mine." He wasn't even sure what was coming out of his mouth anymore. It seemed perfectly sensible in his head a few seconds earlier.

"And none of that matters, Logan. You don't love me. You want nothing to do with me romantically. Remember? You were very clear with your message after the reunion. Painfully clear. I can recite it if you want. It wasn't hard to commit it to memory."

He'd ended it definitively, there was no question about that. Clarity had been for the sake of them both. Of course, he'd never imagined she'd memorize his message. Had he been too cold? "What was I supposed to do? I get to the airport and you're on the cover of a magazine that says sparks were flying when you were auditioning with Derek. That was a week before the reunion and you'd just come off a breakup. That told me everything I needed to know about any future between us."

"There were no sparks with Derek. Why doesn't anyone believe me?"

"There's always some other guy around the corner, isn't there? Some mess of a guy who you can try to fix."

She shot him a final look of disgust before she bolted from the couch and stalked to the front door. "You can be such a jerk. Really. You have an uncanny ability to say the most hurtful things."

He rushed to follow her. "Wait a minute. We're still talking."

She squared her body to his and poked the center of his chest, hard, even though he had a good fifty pounds on her. Maybe more. "If you think the next six months are going to be difficult for you, how do you think the pregnant woman feels? How about the woman who got dumped by both of the men who might've knocked her up? Did you even take two seconds to think about that?"

"I asked you to marry me. I'm willing to play my part."

"You did not ask me to marry you. You were issuing a mandate. And that's not happening, anyway. I'm not marrying someone out of obligation, and certainly not a man who broke up with me. I'm done making mistakes when it comes to you." She opened the door and stormed out. It closed with a *thud* behind her.

Logan turned, his eyes wide open. No way he was

getting any sleep tonight. Julia had given him more than enough to chew on.

His phone beeped with a text. *What now?* He wandered across the room and picked it up from the coffee table. It was from Julia.

We have to leave for the florist by ten.

Great. A whole day of wedding errands with the pregnant woman who drove him crazy, refused to marry him and might be carrying his baby.

Three

Logan had been a royal jerk last night—selfishly worrying how he'd survive the next six months of uncertainty, informing Julia that he expected her to marry him. That was *not* happening. She could do this all on her own. She didn't need help from Logan.

Although she didn't mind the view.

"Oh. Hey. Good morning." He flashed a sheepish smile, standing in the doorway of his room, nothing more than a towel wrapped around his waist, beads of water dotting his shoulder. "I was just getting the paper." Bending over to pick it up, he showed off his perfectly defined back.

Julia stood stuck. His velvety voice delivered a too-sexy memory of their last morning in this hotel— Logan's long, warm naked body pressed against her back in the wee hours, his giving lips on her neck as he slid his hand between her knees, lifted her leg and rocked her world with the most memorable wake-up call, well, ever.

"Jules? You okay?"

"Morning," she sputtered, pushing a room service cart out of her room and into the hall. "I ordered bacon with breakfast, but the smell was making me queasy. If you want the leftovers." *Sexy, Jules. Real sexy.*

He looked both ways, flipped the latch on his door and crossed the hall. He raised the stainless cloche from the plate, grabbing some bacon. "Just two. The camera adds ten pounds."

"You're fine." She stole a glimpse of his stomach, just as hard and muscled as ever. He might not be paid to be an elite athlete anymore, but he maintained his body like one. And to think she'd reaped the benefits—those strapping arms wrapped around her, keeping her close, making her feel for two whole days that she belonged nowhere else. The price of admission had been far more than she'd been willing to pay—every shred of her heart. A big chunk of her pride, too.

"Ready in fifteen?" She braced herself against her door. Being around nearly-naked Logan was making it impossible to stand up straight.

"Definitely. I called down to the valet. We can go out the side entrance. They'll have the car waiting for us."

"You don't think the press will be tipped off by

the eighty-thousand-dollar gleaming black sports car you just had to rent?"

He shrugged. "I'm not about to drive anything less. You'll have to suffer through it, babe."

Babe. As if.

Julia retreated to her room and tried not to obsess over her makeup or hair, but it was hard not to, knowing she'd be spending her day with Logan. He deserved to be tortured by what he'd so solidly rejected. It would likely be her only measure of revenge. She dressed in a swishy navy blue skirt that showed off her legs, black ballet flats and a white sleeveless top with a cut that left her expanding bustline on full display. Boobs. At least she was getting *something* out of this whole single-and-pregnant thing, other than a baby, of course.

She met Logan in the hall, and he just *had* to be stunning. So effortlessly hot in jeans and a white button-down, sleeves rolled up just far enough to again mesmerize her with his inexplicably alluring forearms. He led her out through the side exit and to his rental car. His plan to remain incognito was working perfectly until he peeled out of the parking lot.

"Why did you do that?" Her vision darted back to the hotel entrance. Sure enough, reporters were racing to their cars. "They're following us now." She shook her head. He always had to have his manly moment.

"Don't worry. I'll lose them."

He tried to shake the media as he had the day before, but they got stuck at a red light and he was left to lead a dysfunctional caravan to the florist, with his fancy car front and center. They found their destination a few minutes later, and Julia dashed for the door while Logan took his chance to reprimand the reporters yet again and tell them to stay outside.

Julia swept her hair from her face as a red-haired woman came out of the back with an enormous bucket of flowers blocking her view. "Can I help you?" she asked in a lovely singsong British accent. She plopped her armful onto the checkout counter. "Blimey. You're...her."

Her. Yep. Julia smiled warmly. It was the only way to put people at ease and get them off the subject of who she was. "Hi. You're doing the flowers for my sister Tracy's wedding on Saturday. She asked me to come by and look over everything. She's more than a little picky and I want everything to be perfect for her."

The woman nodded. "Yes. I'm Bryony. And I remember your sister. Very well. Come with me."

The bell on the door jingled as Logan walked inside. With a nod, Julia motioned for him to follow her, and he trailed behind her into a back room. While Bryony pulled buckets of blooms from a cooler, Logan assumed what Julia called his jock-in-command stance—feet nearly shoulder-width apart, hands clasped behind his back, shoulders straight, chest out proud. This was his way of taking in the world. She'd first noticed him doing it their junior year of high school, eyeing him when they played softball in gym class. What a joke that had been—like sending in an Olympic broad jumper to play hopscotch. No one had ever beaned a softball as hard as Logan.

He'd been so far out of her league in school that it took her nearly a year to get up the guts to talk to him, and only after he accidentally showed up at a party at her parents' beach house. Imagine the horror when it dawned on her during that first conversation, as she drank in the mesmerizing beauty of his eyes up close, that he didn't actually know her name. She must have done something right, though...he was her boyfriend a week later.

And when it came to part a year after that, as they both went off to college at far-flung schools, she'd taken the initiative and broken up with him. It had been a bit of a preemptive strike and her attempt to be mature about something. She was terrified to leave home, but she was even more scared of how badly it would hurt when Logan called her from UCLA and said he'd met another girl. Or more likely, another fifty girls. It wouldn't have taken long. In the end, Logan became the guy in her past she couldn't have. That was all there was to it. Circumstances, fate or other women—there was always something standing between them.

Logan waited dutifully next to her while Julia checked the array of flowers set aside for her sister. Her mother's penchant for gardening had left Julia more knowledgeable than the average person. She checked each selection off the list her sister had given her. Hydrangea, snapdragons and roses in white. Pink was for tulips, more roses and... *Oh no.*

"These aren't peonies," Julia said.

"Our supplier was out," Bryony answered. "We had to substitute ranunculus."

Julia shook her head. "No. No. No. Peonies are Tracy's favorite flower. She'll pitch a royal fit if she doesn't have them."

Bryony shrugged. "I'm sorry. That's the best we could do. They aren't that dissimilar."

"Logan, don't you think Tracy's going to be mad about ranunculus?" Julia asked.

"I wouldn't know a ranunculus if it walked up to me and introduced itself." He flashed a wide and clever smile.

The florist tittered like a schoolgirl at Logan's comment. "I'm sorry, but I can't make pink peonies magically appear this time of year. I told your sister there might be a problem getting them."

"I have to fix this." Filled with dread, Julia pulled her phone out of her purse and dialed her assistant, Liz. If Tracy didn't have the right flowers, not only would she freak out, by the transitive property of sisterly blame, it'd be Julia's fault.

"Julia. Is everything okay?" Liz answered.

"Hey. I need you to do something for me. Can you call your flower guy and have four dozen stems of pale pink peonies overnighted to the florist in Wilmington? We need a very pale pink. Not rosy. Not vibrant. Does that make sense?"

"Yes. Of course. I'm on it."

"I'll text you the address. And make sure he knows it's for my sister. I need this to go off without a hitch."

"Got it. Anything else?"

Julia felt as if it was now okay to exhale. "That's it for now."

"Is everything else going okay? The press is really hammering you on this Derek thing, aren't they? And I saw you're hanging out with Logan. How's that going?"

Liz had worked for Julia for years. She might've heard her complain and wax poetic about Logan a few dozen times. Or a few hundred. "Oh, um, it's been fine." She couldn't say more, not with Logan in such close proximity.

"You know, if you wanted the press to go away, you could tell them that you're with Logan," Liz said. "They'll run off and speculate about it for at least a day or two. Or they'll turn it into more of a spectacle. Hard to know, but my gut is they'll take pictures, write their stories and hound Derek with questions about being heartbroken."

Julia watched Logan as he chatted up Bryony, who was blushing like crazy. If any man knew how to make a woman feel good about herself, it was Logan. His presence alone—just breathing the same air he did—made a girl feel special. Precisely why it hurt so much when he took it away. "Well, that's one idea. I'll think about it. Thanks. You're the best."

Julia hung up and took the florist's business card, texting the address to Liz. "The peonies will be here tomorrow morning. Everything else looks great. Thanks for your help."

She turned to Logan. He had the funniest look on

his face—both bewildered and amused. She loved that expression, although if she were honest, she loved everything about his face—full lips shaping his effortless smile, square chin with a tiny scar obscured by scruff, and eyes so warm and sincere it was hard to imagine him ever doing something hurtful.

"Your sister is really lucky she didn't put me in charge of this," he said. "I mean really lucky. Imagine how horrified she'd be if she ended up with ranun... you know. Those flowers."

Julia granted him a quiet laugh. "Ranunculus. And you know how much I love my sister. I'm just trying to make the mess I made a little better. Now let's go deal with the cake."

The throng of reporters outside had grown. Either Julia was losing her patience or they were getting pushier. Logan made sure she got into the car safely, making her truly thankful to have him there. On the way to the bakery, she stole a glimpse of his handsome profile, allowing herself to think about what would've happened last night if he'd proposed for real, because he loved her. If he'd never called it off. If the baby was his. They could hold hands, they could stay up late talking for hours, they could make *plans*. Perhaps that was why she was so dead-set on making everything perfect for her sister. If she couldn't have the fairy tale, at least her sister could.

Fifteen minutes later, they arrived at the bakery and again had to sprint for the door as reporters shouted at them. They seemed to be at the end of their rope. There was much speculation about the reasons why

Julia was running around town with Logan Brandt and not Derek. Not good.

Inside, one of the bakers led them to the work space where all three cakes were being decorated—one for the rehearsal dinner, the groom's cake and of course, the grand, three-tiered wedding cake. Julia took pictures with her phone and sent them to her sister. She got a quick response that, to Julia's great relief, everything except one of the shades of pink frosting passed muster. After straightening that out, and double-checking the delivery times and addresses, she crossed the bakery visit off the list.

She and Logan stood at the bakery window. The reporters were waiting, clogging the sidewalk out front. Logan was finishing a cookie he'd talked out of the girl working behind the counter.

"What happened to 'the camera adds ten pounds'?" Julia asked as he wiped crumbs from the corner of his mouth.

"I will always relax the rules for a chocolate chip cookie. It's my one weakness." He cleared his throat. "Well, that, and my desire to pop one of these reporters in the mouth."

"I don't even want to go out there." Julia hitched her purse up onto her shoulder.

He rolled his neck to the side as if working out a kink. "I don't know if I can take an entire weekend of this. I'm tempted to just tell them I'm your boyfriend to get them to go away."

Exactly what Liz suggested. "It might work," Julia muttered. Of course then she'd have to live with the story. And the myriad ways in which her sister would pitch a conniption. "I'd say we could go out through the alley, but we're still going to have to walk right past them to get to the car."

He took her hand. "It'll be okay. I won't let anything bad happen." He opened the door and out they went, back into the belly of the beast.

They narrowly escaped the reporters outside the bakery unscathed. One of them, a brutish man with a camera lens so long that Logan wondered whether he was compensating for some shortcoming, had become particularly curt with his questions. It was clear he just wanted an answer. And Logan was inclined to agree, only because he himself had reached the boiling point.

Now they were being followed in the car again. "Maybe it's better if you just say something, Jules. The only thing you seem to be accomplishing is frustrating them."

"I wouldn't even know how to say it. You know me. Give me a script and I can deal with it. In front of cameras, with unfriendly faces barking at me, I get panicky. The next thing you know I'm tripping over my words and accidentally telling the press I'm pregnant. And I'll have to spill the beans then. I'm a terrible liar."

"That's probably an argument for just telling your parents about the baby before you mess up and the secret comes out."

"No way. As long as you keep your end of the bargain and keep your mouth shut, it'll be fine."

"Personally, I don't think it's a risk worth taking. Just tell them. Then you can relax and enjoy the wedding."

Julia directed a piercing glare at him. "That's the most harebrained thing you've ever said. My plan is not only the best plan, it's the only plan. My baby. My plan."

Her plan. Jules was doing what she always did—putting her head down, forging ahead and ignoring what everyone else said. Like a beautiful steamroller. She was far better at handing out advice than taking it, which would make it impossible to change her mind. "And what exactly is the rest of your plan? What are you going to say to your parents about the baby's father?"

"I'm going to have to tell them the truth. You might be the dad. And you might not."

Hearing her say that didn't sting any less today than it had last night. "Have you taken the time to think about how they're going to react? Because there could be a lot of fallout, and I'm sorry, but most of that is going to fall on me."

"You have to make everything about you, don't you?"

"No. I don't. I'm just thinking this through to its logical conclusion. Do you remember what your dad asked me the night I took you to senior prom?"

Her eyes narrowed. "What does that have to do with anything?"

"Just answer the question. Do you remember what he said?"

She reached into her bag, pulled out a lip balm and rolled it across her lips. Logan was thankful he was driving and only caught a glimpse of what she was doing. He had a soft spot for her mouth, especially for the things it could do to him.

"My dad asked you what your intentions were with his daughter. Doesn't every dad ask that?"

"Maybe in old movies, they do. My point is that your dad is an old-fashioned guy. And that's part of what I love about him. He's going to want to know if I'm accepting my responsibility. And I told you I'm willing to do that."

"Logan. You dumped me three months ago." She turned sideways in her seat and confronted him. "*Dumped* me."

He didn't want to feel remorseful about ending things with Julia, but he was starting to. Even though he was also certain that they wouldn't have made it through the summer. Julia would've gotten flighty. She would've started doing the things that made him question whether she wanted to be with him, and he never handled that well. "But that was before the baby."

"Precisely the reason this won't work. A baby is not a reason to be together. And I'm not going to be with some man who didn't want me three months ago, just because he's worried about what my dad might think."

"A child deserves two parents." It bothered him to

hear his voice crack like that. A few words and the pain of losing his dad returned to the center of his chest, just as it had the night before. After all these years, it hadn't gotten easier; there were merely longer stretches of time when he could focus on other things. It was hard enough to think about how difficult it'd been on his mom to shoulder the responsibility of three boys, a mortgage and law school. It was even more difficult to recall the promise he'd made at the age of twelve, to his father, his hero, as he slipped away. *Don't worry. I'll be the man of the house. I'll take care of Mom and my brothers.* "I have to accept my responsibility. I owe you that much, and I won't allow your dad to think anything less."

Logan pulled up to the curb out in front of the Keyses' house. The reporters were parking their vans and cars. They'd be descending on them in no time. "We have to make a run for it, Jules. Now."

She gathered her things. Logan hopped out of the car and hurried around to Julia's side. They squeezed past the reporters, walking upstream against a rush of people coming at them. The obnoxious man with the big camera elbowed his way next to Julia, butting into her with his shoulder. The woman behind him pushed ahead. Too many people. On a narrow sidewalk flanked by parked cars and azalea bushes.

Julia stumbled. Her fingers splayed to brace her fall. Her purse flew out of her hand. Muscle memory took over. Logan lunged like an outfielder going for the ball. He curled his arm around Julia, pulling her into him. Everyone came to an abrupt stop.

"Are you okay?" he gasped. Adrenaline surged through his veins. That was too close. She could've been hurt. The baby could've been hurt.

She shook like a leaf, telling him exactly how rattled she was. "I'm okay."

"Don't move." He plucked her purse from the sidewalk and handed it to her. Turning back, he positioned himself directly between Julia and the reporters. He spread his arms wide. If they were going to come another step closer to her, they'd have to go through him. He set his sights on the reckless cameraman. "If you come within fifty feet of her again, you're going to be a very unhappy guy." *More like you're going to be in traction.*

The man puffed out his chest. "Are you threatening me? The sidewalk is a public right-of-way. We have the right to ask questions."

If only there weren't so many cameras trained on him. Two minutes and this guy would know not to get in Julia's face again. Reluctantly, Logan lowered his arms. He hated to do it, but he had to back down or this would escalate. He couldn't manage to unclench his balled fists, though. "Why don't you show some decorum? We're here for a wedding."

"Yesterday she was linked with one of the biggest stars in Hollywood, and now she's at her sister's wedding with her old boyfriend, one of the most successful athletes of the last decade. You can't blame us for wanting to know what's going on."

"Julia, just tell us if you dumped Derek for Logan and we'll leave you alone," one reporter shouted.

"Yeah. Just tell us," another voice chimed in. "Are you cheating on Derek? Is that why he's not with you for your sister's wedding?"

Oh hell no. Cheating? With him? Steam was about to pour out of Logan's ears. He turned back to Julia. The color had been sapped from her face. She looked so defenseless, not at all the self-assured woman he knew. All he could think about was the other helpless person in the middle of this—the baby. God, he'd been an ass last night. Julia was stuck at the center of two crises—Derek and the pregnancy—and he'd let his ego get in the way. The question of paternity was painful for him, but she had to live with much more. He did an abrupt about-face. "Julia and I are together. We're a couple. There's nothing with Derek."

For a second, everyone shut up. Then came a single question. "Is it serious?"

He had to act. And he had to say yes. What kind of man says he isn't serious about the woman he got pregnant? Once the baby news got out, that would be the media's logical assumption. "Yes. It's serious. Now leave us alone, please. Her sister is getting married and the family would like some peace."

"Give us a kiss for the cameras first," one of the reporters said. "So we know it's real."

"Don't push it," left Logan's lips before he realized what he was saying. He couldn't help it. Telling the press no was his gut instinct. And a kiss? As if his feelings weren't confused enough. Not that he didn't want to kiss her. He'd spent a good deal of time in her parents' living room yesterday wishing he could do exactly that. Before things got complicated. Again.

The reporters complained and grumbled. *Just a kiss and we're out of here.*

He was about to tell them to forget it when delicate fingers slipped into his hand. *Julia.* He turned. A sweet smile crossed her face. The color had returned to her cheeks. Although by the way she was now gripping his hand, he was fairly certain the flush was anger, not acquiescence.

"If you guys promise to let my sister get married in peace, you can have your kiss. But you have to promise." The words were for the reporters, but she directed them at Logan. Her lips—the lips he'd fixated on so many times, were waiting right there for him. Pouty and plump.

We promise.

He didn't risk waiting another second, threading his arm around her waist. He witnessed the graceful closing of her eyes and took that as his cue to do the same, to shut out the press and tune out everything around them. When it was Julia and him, all alone, things could be right. It was the rest of the world that made things complicated. Her lips sweetly brushed his—a hint of warmth and sugar, enough to make the edges of his resolve melt and trickle away.

Pressing against her, he felt the newness between them. There was no visible baby bump yet, but there was undoubtedly something new there—a slight, firm protrusion of her belly. That hadn't been there at the beginning of the summer. New life. Was the baby his? Could it bring Julia back to him? Could it bring him back to Julia? Could he really get past that feeling that things would never be right between them?

Just like that, Julia ended the kiss and stepped away, turning toward the house. There was no sentiment, no moment of recognition for what had happened between them.

Logan cleared his throat, trying to conceal how disoriented he was. He was as thrown for a loop by her choice of tactics with the media as he was by his own. Julia, and that kiss, had turned his thinking upside down. "There you go, guys. I expect you to hold up your end of the deal." He turned to Julia and grasped her elbow to usher her ahead, but she stood frozen on the sidewalk. He caught the surprise on her face as she stared ahead at her parents' front porch. He followed her line of sight. The whole family was standing there—Mr. and Mrs. Keys, Tracy and Carter. Judging by their expressions, they'd heard—and seen—it all.

There were car doors closing and engines starting behind him. Probably the vultures on their way to the closest Wi-Fi hotspot to break the news. Or in reality, his little white lie.

"Tell me you didn't just start what I think you did," Julia muttered under her breath, smiling and waving at her parents.

Logan adopted the same phony grin and began walking up the sidewalk, squeezing Julia's hand.

"Tell me you didn't just do what I think *you* did. A kiss?"

"What about you? It's serious?"

His pulse was thumping, but he was sure he'd done the right thing. Mostly sure, at least. "I didn't have a choice," he mumbled. "Somebody was going to get hurt. You were going to get hurt. I had to make them go away. And you're worried about ruining your sister's wedding. That was going to ruin your sister's wedding."

Four

Tracy wasted no time letting her opinion be known. "Nice job making my big weekend all about you." She whipped around and stormed into the house.

Logan grimaced and shrugged, apparently at a loss for words. Julia wasn't doing much better. She was too busy trying to get her bearings after the kiss.

We're together?

This was a bad idea.

Fake romance or real, there would be no opening of those old wounds.

And yet here she was, holding Logan's hand, scaling the stairs to the wraparound porch and filing inside her parents' house. Logan closed the door after her, while her father clapped him on the shoulder.

The grin on her dad's face was as wide as the

beach at low tide. "Sounds like I'll be marrying off a second daughter soon. Julia's mother and I had always hoped this day would come."

Married? Good God, what was it with the men in Julia's life assuming marriage was the next logical step? "Dad, isn't that a little presumptuous?"

"The man said serious. What else am I to presume?"

"We're so happy, Jules. We've always thought Logan was the only one for you." Her mother's ability to radiate warmth and happiness made everything worse. How would her parents feel when she told them her secret on Sunday? Would they only be happy for her if Logan was indeed the dad? Precisely the reason she didn't want a paternity test. She didn't want her baby to be judged because of who his or her father might be. It was such an old-fashioned fixation, anyway. She could be a mom on her own, with no need for a man. The baby was Julia's, and that was all anyone needed to know.

Julia sucked in a deep breath, not knowing what to say. Logan had put them in a horrible position. And admittedly, Julia had probably made it worse with the kiss, but the press had said they'd go away. She wanted that insurance. Still, playing fast and loose with the truth… Julia might be an actress, but she sucked at lying. "Logan and I aren't together. He just said that to make the press go away."

"I knew it!" Tracy exclaimed, breaking her momentary silence. "At least Logan cared enough about

me to do something about the problem." She shot Julia
a pointed stare. "Unlike my sister."

"What about the kiss? That's what really made
them go away."

Logan nodded in agreement. "True. The kiss was
definitely Julia's idea."

Don't remind me.

"The kiss was fake?" Her mother's voice was rife
with distress, just as it had been the day before when
this all started. "No. It couldn't have been. It was so
sweet. It looked real."

I bet. Julia still felt that kiss all over every inch of
her body. Damn Logan and his resolve-destroying
lips. "It was just what they asked for. A kiss for the
cameras. Nothing else. I am a halfway decent actress, you know."

Julia had thought she'd have to fake her way
through it, that she was still too mad at Logan for
the way he'd treated her. That wasn't the way it had
gone at all. The second his lips fell on hers, her body
cast aside any hurt feelings and went for it. Her trai-
torous mouth knew exactly what to do, and sought
his warmth and touch, his impossibly tender kiss.
Her body knew how perfectly they fit together, physically at least, and was all too eager to find a way for
them to squeeze three months of lost time into a few
short heartbeats.

Logan stepped forward. "Actually, it's not entirely
true that Julia and I aren't together."

If Julia could've clamped her hand over Logan's
mouth and make it look like an accident, she would

have. Tracy threw up her hands, stomped once on the hardwood floor with her jeweled beachcomber sandal and began pacing the room. "Which is it? Will you two get your act together so we can go back to enjoying my wedding week?"

And to think that earlier today, Julia's big concern had been shades of pink frosting. Now she was far more worried about shades of red. Namely the various hues of crimson coloring her sister's face. Volcano Tracy was about to blow.

"I spent the last six months worrying about everything that could go wrong," Tracy continued, circling the room. "Would the church put us down for the wrong date? Would I find the perfect dress? Would the caterer serve fish instead of chicken? I never imagined that the person who would ruin it would be my own sister. You just can't let me have the spotlight. You *have* to create all of this drama. You can't live without it, can you?"

Julia's father stuffed his hands into the pockets of his flat-front khakis. "Now wait a minute, Trace. We're just having a conversation. Your mother and I would like to know what exactly is going on with Logan and Julia."

Yeah, Dad. Get in line.

"Julia and I had a long talk last night about…" Logan started, looking over to Julia as if he was waiting for her to say that now was a good time to come out with the baby news, which it absolutely was not.

Julia felt as though she was going to be sick. She

tried to send him direct messages with her eyes. *One word and I'll never speak to you again.*

"Julia and I had a long talk about things," Logan finished, scratching his head. "No one should put the idea of Julia and me, together, out of the realm of possibility."

Julia would've let out a massive sigh of relief about the baby secret still being under wraps if she weren't so annoyed. The two of them together was out of all realms. She'd wasted enough of her life on men who didn't love her.

The smirk on Tracy's face showed zero amusement. She wagged her finger in the air. "Oh no. I'm calling BS on this. Jules, you told me you two were done. And with good reason, remember? I didn't spend all those hours on the phone listening to you cry for nothing."

Tracy had indeed clocked a lot of time listening to her sob into the phone. She knew Julia and Logan's long history, the one that had taken its first horrible turn when Julia broke up with Logan before they both went off to college. Tracy had listened to Julia complain year after year about the women Logan was linked to in the tabloids—always models, always stunning and perfect, one of them even becoming his fiancée for a short time. Even though his engagement hadn't lasted, it ate at Julia like crazy, and Tracy had to suffer right along with her sister. Tracy knew exactly how dysfunctional they were together.

"Tracy Jean. I don't know why you'd be so rude to your sister," their mother said.

"Come on, hon." Carter walked up behind Tracy and set his hands on her shoulders. "Why don't you and I go in the kitchen and get a nice, cold drink?"

Tracy shrugged her way out of Carter's grip. "Oh, please. I love you, but you don't see what's going on, and you're yet another person who thinks Logan can do no wrong. And Mom, don't even start with rude. All I'm saying is that Julia and Logan have zero business being together. That ship has sailed. I mean, seriously, Jules? After what happened after the reunion?"

Well, then. Was Tracy about to air Julia's dirty laundry in front of their parents? Julia's mind raced for diversion tactics. If only an earthquake could hit the coast of North Carolina right now. Or a hurricane, at least.

"Did I miss something?" Julia's father asked.

Logan cleared his throat and bugged his eyes at Julia. As if that was going to help her figure a way out of this mess. Or keep Tracy's mouth from running. Sweat dripped down Julia's back, part nervousness, part the iron fist her dad used to rule the thermostat. "Dad, can we please turn on the air-conditioning?"

"Julia and Logan slept together," Tracy blurted, not giving her dad a chance to answer. "And then he dumped her."

Julia braced for a gasp of disgrace from her mother or a disapproving grunt from her father.

"I'm sorry to hear that," Julia's mother said. "But couples have rough patches. You and Carter should know that better than anyone. You two broke up for an entire year before you got back together and got engaged."

"You're both smart. I'm sure you'll work everything out," their father said, easing into his wingback chair as casually as if they'd all been discussing where to go to dinner.

I'll be damned. That in itself was pure evidence of how much her parents adored Logan. Talk of premarital sex—words spoken out loud, in the living room of the scandal-free state senator from New Hanover County and his wife no less, and not a judgmental peep came from either of them.

"This really doesn't seem like a topic for polite conversation," Julia said. *Or even impolite conversation.* "Let's get back to focusing on the wedding. Logan got the press to go away. Let's be thankful for that."

Tracy arched her eyebrows and cracked a fake smile. "The only way it stays that way is if you two put on a convincing show. For everyone. The wedding guests, the people at your hotel. All of our friends and family. They can't all be in on your little lie, or it'll just get out and that will bring back the press with a vengeance."

Oh no. Julia's stomach sank. Tracy was right. They couldn't trust anyone beyond these four walls with the truth. Julia didn't even want to think about the return of those awful reporters, especially the guy with the big lens. They were going to have to put on a show. A convincing show of love and affection and romance. Great. Julia sighed. If that was what it would take, then fine. For now, she only wanted peace and calm. And somewhere to sit. And maybe a cheeseburger.

Her grandmother's antique cuckoo clock in the foyer chimed three o'clock, which really meant it was two thirty. The thing had never worked right. "The afternoon is wasting away. Trace, don't you and I have a date to decorate the beach house for the rehearsal dinner? It's our only real chance for sisterly bonding this weekend." *And I can un-ruffle a million feathers.*

"Honestly, Jules, you ruined it. I need a nap so I can calm down. I'm worried I might strangle you if we spend any time alone."

Julia swallowed, hard. That certainly clarified things. "Okay. I understand."

"Tell you what," Logan interjected. "Jules and I will take care of the decorating."

There he goes. Logan Brandt to the rescue.

"That would be wonderful," her mother said. "Plus, it sounds like it'll be good for you two to have some alone time."

Alone time. Good Lord.

"Happy to do it," Logan said.

"Yep." Julia nodded. Speaking as little as possible seemed like the only way to make a graceful exit from this house. Her entrance had been anything but.

After a quick trip to the bathroom, Julia joined Logan in the car, and they were on their way to perform their new wedding duties.

"I'm starving." Julia tore open the wrapper on a protein bar she'd stuck in her purse. Her stomach rumbled, but gladly accepted the sustenance. "And this isn't going to be enough. I need real food."

Logan nodded, surveying the road ahead, a wide stretch of shopping plazas, gas stations and eateries. "Unless you want to find a sit-down restaurant, your options are chain fast food or biscuits."

Ooh. The dilapidated sign for Sunset Biscuit Kitchen was straight ahead. It'd been years since she'd eaten there. It wasn't exactly camera-friendly cuisine, but her pregnant appetite had her salivating at the thought of their fluffy, buttery pieces of heaven. "Biscuits."

"I was hoping you'd say that." Logan pulled into the parking lot of the restaurant, which was really more like a shack, with a battleship-gray exterior and a faded red roof. There was no drive-through or dining room—just a walk-up window and if memory served, lightning-fast service. "The usual? Fried chicken biscuit and a hash brown?"

"How do you remember this stuff?"

"I remember everything."

That was indeed her standard, very unhealthy order. But she wanted more than that. "Can you also get me a sausage and egg biscuit? And an extra biscuit with honey? You know. Just in case."

Logan nodded and smiled. "I like this whole pregnant and hungry thing. It's adorable."

"Adorable?"

"It's a nice change of pace. I spend entirely too much time with women who order side salads and nothing else."

As if Julia wanted or needed the vision of Logan's penchant for supermodels planted in her head. "Yeah, well, I'm going to have to spend every waking minute in the gym after this baby is born. But for now, I want to eat everything."

"I'm on it. One order of everything, coming up."

Logan hopped out of the car and strolled up to the ordering window. Maybe it was the aftershocks of the kiss, but she had to admire him as he walked away. How could she not? From a purely objective standpoint, one having nothing to do with hurt feelings or history, he was a spectacular specimen.

Luckily, the line wasn't long in the middle of the afternoon. Julia didn't think she could endure much of a wait. Logan was back in a few short minutes, white parchment bag, two bottles of water and a fat stack of paper napkins in hand.

He opted to drive and eat, and they went for an entire fifteen minutes without argument or conflict, Julia's stress level dropping with each artery-clogging but oh-so-delicious bite—crispy buttermilk fried chicken tucked inside a light-as-air biscuit. But then Logan finished his sandwich.

"I can't believe you couldn't keep our secret until we had a chance to talk about it. I had it all worked out and you ruined it."

"Our secret? Oh, no. That was your secret, not mine. You need to have your head examined. You made everything fifty times more complicated."

"I made the press go away, didn't I?"

"Yes. And apparently my parents would like to

present you with a key to the city for doing so. In the meantime, they're going to be that much more confused on Sunday when I tell them about the baby. They're going to be asking themselves what exactly did all of that mean. Especially when you had to tell them that we talked about us last night."

"It doesn't have to be confusing, Jules. If you'd think about reality for a minute and realize that I'm your best shot at giving the baby a real father."

She knew for a fact he wasn't thinking straight. He was letting his macho brain run the show, and that never went well. He was relishing the idea of being her knight in shining armor, and although she appreciated the gesture, she knew how empty a promise it was. As soon as he realized the reality of what he was saying, of what he was getting into, he'd take it back. And then where would she be? Right where she was the last time he rejected her.

Plus, she knew Logan. He hated every guy who had come along after him. Every last one. There was no way he would want to play Dad if it turned out that her ex was the father. She always stopped herself before she got much further in her thinking, wondering what that moment would be like. It was better for her to think of the baby only as hers—50 percent of her DNA, 100 percent of her heart. Julia wouldn't allow paternity to cloud her feelings for her child. Her future was the baby, making it work, finding happiness in what would become the new normal. Mother and child. Everyone else could worry about themselves.

"Right now, I'm focused on the only thing I can

control, which is being a good mother. I can't afford to depend on anyone else, especially not a man."

"It's not a sign of weakness to count on someone."

"I'm not worried about how it might look if I agree with you. I'm worried about how bad it would feel if and when you changed your mind. Plus, let's not forget the most damning detail."

He stopped at the stoplight that T-boned into Lumina Avenue signaling for the left turn. It was as if they'd turned back the clock thirteen years and he remembered exactly where they were going. "Well? I'm waiting for the most damning detail."

Julia sighed quietly and looked out the car window, admiring the gorgeous shades of pink and purple that colored the edges of the darkening late-afternoon sky. So beautiful. So romantic. "We aren't in love, Logan."

Well, one of us isn't. The realization had been there in her head from the moment she saw him yesterday. Everything she'd convinced herself of over the summer was wrong. She wasn't over him at all. She was just going to have to try harder. It was a matter of survival. Of course, that wasn't going to be easy when they were keeping up their charade for the public and the array of guests at the wedding. She could see it now. Holding hands. Pet names. Kissing. Good God, kissing. How was she supposed to try harder to fall out of love with him at the same time they were expected to kiss? This would require her greatest acting skills. No doubt about that.

"Maybe we just need to figure out a way to fall

back in love," he said, as if the statement was of little consequence.

The mere fact that he suggested they figure it out proved that he didn't love her. No one who was in love found it necessary to figure it out. "You can't force it. Either it's there or it isn't." Talk about a damning detail. If ever there was one, that was it.

Logan slowed down the car and pointed up ahead. "That's it, right?"

"Yep."

"I'm so used to finding it in the dark. I was worried I might not recognize it."

"Well, it just got a new paint job. My parents did some sprucing up for the wedding. I can't wait to see inside. This will be my first time."

Logan turned into the driveway of her parents' beach getaway, the one that had once belonged to her grandparents on her mom's side. The parking area was tucked underneath, the house up on stilts for the times when mid-Atlantic hurricanes lapped an extra twenty feet of water up over the dunes. She opened her car door and a waft of briny ocean, carried on a sticky breeze, hit her nose. It brought with it a wealth of memories, many starring Logan. He pulled plastic bins of party decorations from the trunk, and Julia led the way to the wood stairs up to the front door. Even with a fresh coat of butter yellow on the shaker siding of the house, every sensory cue shuffled images through her mind, like flipping through the pages of an old photo album. With the roar of the waves, the wind catching her hair and having him so near, distant moments felt like yesterday, the most palpable of which were the times when Logan had been her everything. And she had been his.

"You okay, Jules? Carsick again?" Logan was at her side as she paused at the front door with the key in the lock. His hand went to her lower back, true concern in his warm and gentle eyes.

It isn't even funny how not okay I am. She nodded. "Yeah. I'm good. We should probably go inside and get started, huh?"

"No time like the present."

Yes, it was now time to start, right where it all began.

Five

Logan followed Julia into the beach house, hardly believing his own eyes. Was this really the same place? Once dark, cramped quarters, the kitchen seemed nearly twice its original size. It was completely open to the living room thanks to the obliteration of an entire wall, the space crowned with high-beamed whitewashed ceilings. Where there had once been dark cabinets, wood paneling and avocado-green appliances sat their modern-day counterparts in white and stainless steel. "Your parents practically gutted the place. It looks incredible."

Julia nodded, appearing pleased as she admired the room. She ran her hand along the edge of the gleaming marble countertop on the center island, another new addition. "It does look great, doesn't it? I really hope Tracy's happy with it."

In Logan's estimation, Tracy was a complete brat if this didn't show her just how hard her family was trying to make her wedding as perfect as could be. "She'd better be happy. She'd better be thanking your parents for days."

Julia wandered into the living room, past a sprawling white sectional couch. Judging by the immaculate upholstery, it was brand-new. The old brick fireplace had undergone a makeover of stacked stone, topped with a distressed wood mantel hosting an array of framed family photos. He was oddly thankful for the considerable house renovation. It took an edge off the memories. It was difficult enough to be here with her, trying hard to keep from kicking up the dust of old memories, all while dealing with the issues of the present.

"How'd your parents afford to do this? There's no way a state senator makes a big salary, and your mom's a teacher." Logan joined her at the expanse of glass doors at the far side of the room that led to the sprawling deck. White rocking chairs pitched forward and back in the wind.

"They didn't afford it. When Tracy told me she wanted to get married here and that Mom and Dad were going to take out a second mortgage to spruce it up, I just sent a check. It seemed silly for them to be spending money on this."

"Wait a minute. I thought they were just doing the

rehearsal dinner here. The ceremony's in town at the church down the street from the River Room, isn't it?"

"Yes. As soon as Tracy realized how hard it'd be to wear heels in the sand, she changed her mind about getting married on the beach."

"You spent tens of thousands of dollars so your sister could have a nice place for a rehearsal dinner and not have to worry about her shoes?"

"You haven't seen the shoes. They're really cute." She grinned and shrugged it off. "This is as much for my parents as anything. They're so close to retirement. I wanted to do something nice for them."

Julia wasn't one of the most generous people Logan had ever met, she was *the* most generous. Logan had been on the receiving end of her generosity many times, especially when it came to advice and support. If you called Julia in the middle of the night, she'd answer. And she'd listen, no matter how long it might take to unravel a problem. It was a wonderful quality, but it also meant people took advantage of her. Especially men.

Had Logan taken advantage in June? That night when she was a damning mix of long legs and a laugh that was like truth serum? That night when she was all open ears and sympathy? That night when her touch electrified him and reminded him that busted baseball career or not, he was still alive? "That was awfully nice of you. You'd think Tracy would lay off the extra-demanding routine considering all of that."

"It's her big day. I get it. It doesn't matter what I

did last week or last month to help out. Right now is what matters, and she wants it to be perfect."

Julia stared off at the surf as if she were hypnotized. Daylight was fading, coloring the sky with a swirl of pink and orange that only made her more radiant. It wouldn't be long until the moon would be making its appearance on the horizon; night would be falling. They'd be all alone in this beautiful house, no one expecting them anywhere, all while his body persisted in sending potent reminders of the kiss they'd shared mere hours ago.

He cleared his throat. If he thought for too long about her lips on his, he might do something stupid—namely acting like they could kiss without hurting each other. "And you want to give that to her."

"My sister and I fight, but we love each other a lot. We still talk almost every day."

Precisely the reason why Tracy knew what had happened at the reunion. "So I gathered by her reaction to the idea of you and me together."

She shook her head, seemingly bringing herself back to reality. Without so much as looking at him, she headed back to the kitchen island and began pulling party supplies out of the bins. "I had to tell somebody. I was pretty wrecked by the whole thing."

He'd been so certain at the time that it was the right call. Now, alone with her, part of him wanted somebody to smack him upside the head. Regardless of right or wrong, no matter if it had been smart to want to save himself, he'd messed up. "I'm sorry, Jules. Really, I am. It was never my intention to hurt you."

She shot him a look of pure skepticism, then unloaded strands of Christmas lights. "You knew it was going to hurt. I don't buy it for a minute that you didn't know that."

He *had* known that, but in the heat of the moment, angry that their frustrating past was repeating itself again, he hadn't worried about it much. "I figured you'd get over it pretty quickly. It's not like you don't have a million guys falling at your feet."

She chuckled, but it wasn't in fun. "Oh, please. Remind me to call you the next time I'm sitting around at home with absolutely zero guys at my feet. It happens all the time."

He had to stop himself from unleashing his own laugh. She was deluded about what she could have if she'd just settle on one person. "That's a choice you make and you know it. As soon as you finally decide you want to be with one person, you'll have no problem."

The look of hurt that crossed her face made him wish he could take back his words, even though they had been the reality, and something she needed to hear. "That's hilarious coming from you. And I haven't decided anything. The men in my life have a real talent for making those decisions before I have a clue what's going on."

"Probably because they're the wrong men."

"Probably." She crossed her arms, pressing her lips together tightly, telling him without words that she considered him a member of the group of men labeled "wrong."

"Oh, come on. I'm not like those guys. It's not the same thing at all. What you and I had was different."

"Is it really that different? You think it's some special snowflake? Because the end result is the same. I'm on my own. Except this time I have a baby to worry about."

"You're just being stubborn about that. I told you I'd accept my responsibility."

Her jaw immediately tensed. Normally that might make him worry that he'd angered her, but the truth was it made her lower lip jut out in a very sexy way. So he'd take it. Her eyes blazed and she balled up her hands. That wasn't quite as sexy. She grabbed a roll of streamers and nailed a sofa cushion with it.

"Nice throw."

"I was imagining the couch was your face."

"Oh." He kneaded his forehead. He no longer had to wonder how mad he was making her.

She closed her eyes and took a breath so deep her shoulders rose to her ears. "Can we please talk about something else? After everything else today, I really don't want to get into this right now."

Logan stuffed his hands into his pants pockets, fighting his own brand of frustration. The circles he and Jules could talk in had worn a hole in his psyche. He didn't have the mettle to push her more tonight if it would only lead to an argument. "Fine."

"Let's focus on the wedding." She returned to rummaging through the box. "Make yourself useful and get the stepladder. I think it's in the laundry room."

"I'll be right back."

He wound his way down the hall past the bedrooms to the laundry room in the back corner of the house. This space hadn't seen much of a makeover aside from a fresh coat of white paint and what appeared to be a new washer and dryer.

Feeling nostalgic about a laundry room was odd for sure, but he and Jules had once had a pretty epic, albeit brief, make-out session in this exact place. He'd been invited over for a family cookout and bonfire a few weekends after they became boyfriend and girlfriend. Julia had spilled mustard on her top and was headed inside to change and treat the stain. After an exchange of pointed glances, Logan had gone with her, saying he needed to use the bathroom. With her parents watching their every move, they'd both known it was likely the only time alone they would get. She'd practically slammed the door shut once they were inside the laundry room. *I need to take my shirt off or this stain will never come out.* Logan had never before been thankful for an accidental condiment spill.

His hand had been up her shirt before then, but that moment had been different. He could finally see her—every beautiful vulnerability. They'd known they only had about five minutes before Julia's very observant father came looking for her. They'd made the most of it—frantic kisses against the door, tongues winding, hands everywhere. It took Logan hours to cool off that night, and he couldn't help but lie in bed when he got home and think about Julia and how perfect she was and how lucky he was that she was his girlfriend.

A few days later they had sex for the first time. Julia had been a virgin, making him that much more nervous. He hadn't been particularly experienced, either. After that, their young love had grown so fast it was as if it had been rushing to fill the corners of the universe. Every day was magical, even when they fought, which was often. Even so, they'd been incapable of getting enough of each other. Never enough.

Just thinking about how all-consuming it had once been was a little overwhelming, since it eventually led to unhappy memories. It had been such a shock to the system when Julia ended it. The girl who had lifted him out of the fog of losing his dad had removed herself from his life. Of course he'd kept a stiff upper lip that day, playing it off, agreeing that it was for the best. What else could he have done? They were both going off to college. And everyone had preached to them for months that high school sweethearts never made it long-distance.

He took a deep breath, stopping himself from exploring this train of thought. The past was only clouding up the here and now, and he only had a few days to convince her they needed a solid plan. If the baby was his, he was not about to be the guy negotiating weekends and joint custody.

He found the stepladder in the corner storage closet and brought it out to Julia. "You put on some music," he noted.

"You and I could use the distraction." Julia fanned a piece of paper in the air. "Tracy drew up a schematic of how she wants the room decorated."

"Wow." Logan studied the drawing, which had all the specifics about where streamers and strands of lights were to go. He hadn't seen such attention to detail since the team manager laid out the team strategy for game seven of the World Series. "Seems like we could've paid someone to do all of this."

"This was supposed to be my quality time with my sister. And honestly, she's way too much of a control freak."

Runs in the family. "It's a lot of work for a cookout for the wedding party and family."

"Doesn't matter. As big sister and maid of honor, I'm obliged to carry out her wishes." Julia handed Logan the trail end of a string of lights. "As best man, you are similarly obliged. So let's get to work."

Logan followed orders, scooting the ladder all over the room, moving furniture when needed, and looping lights and streamers as instructed.

"How's the new job going?" Julia asked, carefully looking over his work. "I have to say the wardrobe department puts you in some pretty interesting ties."

He wasn't sure how he felt about the fact that all she'd noticed was what he was wearing. At least she'd tuned in. "Do you watch often?"

"Every now and then. If I'm flipping through the channels."

"So I'm not a destination so much as something

you pass by." The irony of that statement wasn't lost on him.

"What about you? How many of my movies have you seen in recent history?"

Logan didn't watch Julia's movies. The reigning queen of romantic comedies, she almost always had at least one on-screen kiss and sometimes even a bedroom scene. He couldn't handle that. Pretend or not, even when she wasn't his, the idea of her with another man made him crazy. "You know me. I don't get to the movies."

"That's such a lousy excuse. They're all on TV. *Losing Mr. Wonderful* is practically on a continual cable loop." She shook her head in dismay. "And you're just avoiding my question. Do you like your new job?"

Yes, Logan had deflected on this subject. It wasn't that he hated his job so much as it wasn't the same. It wasn't taking the field and playing. "I like it. It's a challenge. But I'm getting used to it."

Julia handed him another string of lights. "You don't have to try to convince me. I know you better than anyone."

He sucked in a deep breath and climbed a rung higher on the ladder. He didn't want to tell her the truth. It led to a place where she pitied him, and he hated that more than anything. "I don't want to talk about it."

"Logan, just tell me. You know I'm a good listener."

"I know you are. I don't need the advice right now.

I'm fine." He glanced down to see a doubtful smirk cross her face.

"If you don't like your job, you should just quit. Go do something else."

Why had he even bothered to deflect? She wasn't about to let it go. "It's not that. It's that nothing is going to replace baseball. I can't do what I really want to do, and you already know that."

"You know what you should do? You should write a memoir. You've led this amazing life, and you've always been an excellent writer. I'm sure it would be a bestseller." She waltzed off to one of the bins and fished out more bundles of lights.

"See? You're trying to fix my problems. Maybe I don't need you to fix me. Maybe I'm just fine the way I am."

"Why is it so hard for you to accept a little encouragement from me? It's okay to stop being the big, strong man for a few minutes, you know."

"I could ask you the same thing. Why is it so hard for you to accept my help?"

"If you're referring to your offer to marry me, we should agree that it's best if we're just friends."

Friends. Yes. Could they ever get beyond that? Three months ago, his decision had been absolutely not. But that was before the baby. That was before she needed him. Finally, for once, she needed him. "Maybe we could make another try at more than friends." This was a different and softer approach than the one he'd taken last night, one that might actually work if she'd listen.

"Ummm. No." Julia crossed her arms over her chest, then gazed up at the ceiling, scrutinizing his work. "And no to that, too." She pointed at the spot where he'd just hung lights. "Redo that."

"What's wrong with it?"

"They're not looped at the same height as the other ones. It doesn't match."

Logan grumbled and hopped off the ladder to grab a drink of water, partly annoyed by being bossed around by his high school sweetheart about holiday lights. The other part of him bristled over her quick dismissal of the notion of being more than friends. "A few cocktails tomorrow night and no one's going to notice, you know."

"Well, I don't get to drink, so I'll notice." She stepped onto the ladder, grabbing the top rung and making it clear she was on her way up. "I'll do it."

He rushed over to her, not thinking, just reacting. One hand landed on the ladder, the other on her hip. "No, you don't. You are not climbing up there."

She turned in his arms, gorgeous locks of hair cascading around her face. "Oh, please. I'm fine."

He should've stepped back, let her get down from the single step she'd taken, but he didn't want to. His body wanted this. And this was the one part of their chemistry that Julia had a hard time resisting. So let her resist. Let her tell him that she didn't want to at least explore things when he had his arms around her. "You and the baby are not getting hurt. Not on my watch."

"Please promise me you won't accidentally say something like that out loud in front of my family."

"I'm serious, Jules. I'm not kidding around. You and the baby. It's a game changer for us. You can't deny that." He gripped her waist and carefully lifted her, lowering her to the safety of the floor. He didn't let go. The notion of game changers had him wondering how he could ever do the same to her mind. As if fate was trying to give them both a nudge, a song came over the radio that had powerful memories for them both.

Recognition crossed Julia's face and she smiled, pressing her hand to her chest. "This song. Oh my God. I love this song."

The arrival of this song was about as ill-timed as could be. It had been Logan and Julia's make-out song when they were in school. Only a few notes in and Julia was already melting, probably not a good idea considering whose arms she was in. And yet she wasn't really sure she cared that this was a bad idea. After twenty-four hours of painful truths and uncomfortable secrets, it was too easy to give in to the one thing that felt good—Logan's hand at her waist, carefully sliding to her back, as if he was hoping to do it undetected. This was comfortable. Familiar. And she wanted that now more than anything.

He took her hand and began swaying them both back and forth.

"Typically, a guy asks a girl to dance. He doesn't

just launch into it without an invitation." She felt the need to at least feign a protest.

He smiled, sending a trickle of electricity down her spine. "I'm not big on asking. And you'll just say no."

Forget the song—she had little defense for Logan when he was acting like this. Romantic. Slightly bossy. Sexy as all get-out. This was precisely the version of Logan she couldn't resist at the beginning of the summer. This was the Logan who could leave her undone with a single glance. Dancing was the least of her worries—all he had to do was look at her in the right way and she'd be clay in his very capable hands.

"I'm worried about what might happen if there's too much touching."

"It's just a dance. We're taking the room for a spin. Seems like part of our due diligence as best man and maid of honor. We wouldn't want Tracy to tell us tomorrow that something's wrong with the way the lights are strung."

"You're just saying that because I'm trying so hard to keep her happy."

"Okay, then. How about this? You and I have to convince a whole lot of people that we're a couple. Consider it practice."

She couldn't argue with him on that. And at least she felt like she had someone on her side, stuck in her proverbial boat. Where would she be right now if she didn't have Logan? Feeling even more alone than she already did. At least someone knew her secret. And someone understood how she felt about making her sister happy. It was merely an unfortunate coincidence that her ally in secret-keeping and wedding planning also happened to be the man who broke her heart.

Logan continued with the dance, committing to it with a more deliberate sway. He squeezed her hand and pressed into her back with his other hand. Julia admired the handsome and cocky grin on his face as each musical note pulled her further under his spell. It was like his lips were sending her secret messages. *Just another kiss, Jules. You know you loved the one from earlier today.*

His eyes drifted lower, and she couldn't help but be amused by the way he unsubtly ogled her cleavage.

"My eyes are up here, mister."

A guilty smile crossed his lips. "What? It's impossible not to look. I mean, they're right there."

"They've always been right there."

He cocked an eyebrow. "Not like this, they haven't." He shook his head. "Never mind. Forget I said anything."

"No. What were you going to say?"

He pulled her closer, pressing their chests together, his mouth drifting to her ear. "I'm not saying another thing on the subject. I'll just get into trouble." The heat of his breath grazed her neck, sending a rush of warmth through her.

"Fine. Then dance with me." She gave in to the moment, settling her head against Logan's shoulder. He pulled her even closer and held her tight. Side to side, slow and steady, feet moving only slightly, their dance continued into a different song—less meaningful in terms of their shared history, but still laid-back and sexy. His warmth poured into her, wrapping her up in contentment.

"I was thinking about the parties you and Tracy used to have here. The ones your parents didn't know about," Logan said.

"They were fun, weren't they?" So many of her memories of this house were tied to those parties. After Julia had gotten her driver's license, she and Tracy used to sneak the keys to the beach house and invite friends over. Neither girl had been particularly wild, and Julia always insisted the guest list be small and they leave the house immaculate, but they certainly did things they shouldn't have been doing—drinking beer and kissing boys, mostly, although Tracy had far more luck in that department than Julia. That was until the night Logan showed up.

"Of course, I think the first one I came to was the most fun."

She had to smile. "It might have been the best night ever." It had been the best—a huge turning point for her. Emboldened by half a can of light beer, Julia finally had the guts to talk to Logan. She'd been pining for him for more than a year before that. "We talked forever that night."

"A lifetime."

Indeed, they'd had an hours-long conversation out on the dunes, Julia with her knees pulled up to her chin and Logan stretching his legs and digging his feet into the sand. She'd never listened to anyone so eagerly, hanging on every word as Logan told her about losing his dad, about trying to be the man of the family, about baseball. Summer wind swirled, whipping at the beach grass as the roar of the ocean swelled and receded over and over again. It was literally a dream come true… Logan Brandt, the most perfect guy she'd ever laid eyes on, had not only noticed her, he'd talked to her. He'd held her hand. And then, beneath that impossibly beautiful midnight-blue sky, he'd done the thing she'd worried no boy as amazing as Logan would ever want to do. He'd kissed her.

Logan cleared his throat and began trailing his fingers along her spine. It felt so good. Too good. "I know I rambled on and on that night. I was nervous about kissing you."

"I don't believe that for a second. You were so smooth. You've always been the smooth guy."

"Something about you made me question my kissing ability."

She laughed quietly. "You were perfect. Absolutely perfect." Julia could've sworn she floated on air for two days after that first kiss. Even if nothing else had ever happened between them, she could have lived off the memory for a lifetime. When he'd asked her a week later to be his girlfriend? She was so gone, up to her neck in her first love, the then-shy Julia didn't even bother with an answer. She'd thrown her arms around his neck and kissed him like her life depended on it. Was there any better feeling than that? Julia didn't think so, even now. That love had transformed her. It had made her believe that she was lovable. She'd never really been sure of it before that.

"I'm not sure I buy it when you say you felt nothing from our kiss in front of the cameras." Logan's voice was low, resonating throughout her body. It wasn't just the kiss that made her feel something. Everything about him made her feel, and that was a terrifying feeling. Leaving herself open to him eventually led to hurt. Always.

A heavy sigh escaped her lungs. "It was a kiss. It didn't change my world," she lied.

Logan reared back his head and brought their dance to a stop. "I don't believe you."

"They're my feelings. I think I know what I did and did not feel." She tried to avoid his gaze, but he followed her with his, as if he was pleading for a retraction. "Fine. It was a nice kiss. You've always been a good kisser. Is that what you want to hear?"

"I'm not fishing for compliments. I felt something, and I think you did, too. I think you're trying to convince yourself of something that isn't the way it actually happened."

She shrugged, but she didn't like dismissing it. The temptation to give in and tell him how much she'd loved it was too great. He was wearing down her resolve, and she had to put a stop to it. "It was hours ago. I hardly even remember it."

"Then let me refresh your memory."

He clutched her neck and lowered his lips to hers. His mouth was warm and soft. Giving. Like Logan had an unlimited supply of affection and he was going to hand it out like candy. He dictated the pace— languid and dizzying, suggesting they deserved to take their time, and for the moment, she believed they did. Here they were, all alone, in this big empty house, all the time in the world. His mouth drifted to her cheek, his stubble scratching her nose, then he traveled to her jaw and kissed her neck. She kept her eyes closed, luxuriating in every heavenly press of his lips to hers, not wanting it to end.

"Tell me you don't feel anything," he whispered into her ear.

"I don't feel anything." She reasoned that she was merely following orders, but she'd actually become a fountain of fibs. She was surprised her nose wasn't growing. The truth was that she was feeling everything right now. Her entire body was so alert she could probably stay awake for the next twenty-four hours.

"You said it yourself earlier today. You're a terrible liar."

And you're a ridiculously good kisser. "I know what I said. You don't have to remind me."

Six

The ride back to the hotel was long. And quiet. Part of Julia was glad she'd had the sense to lie to him and pull them back from the precipice before bodies slipped out of clothes. And her sense slipped out of her brain. The other part of her, the hormonal part, was downright annoyed. She'd been in the arms of an eager Logan and she'd said she felt nothing. She'd lied and denied herself sex, all in the same breath. They could've christened the brand-new sofa. Regret was starting to needle her.

Focus on the baby. That was her key to keeping Logan where he belonged—in the strangest friend zone she could imagine. She had to keep her life in order for the sake of the baby. A child needed stability and normalcy. Allowing herself to be tangled up with yet another man who didn't love her was a recipe for anything but what she wanted to give her baby.

Logan pulled up in front of the hotel, and thankfully the press had kept their promise. They'd stayed away. Finally, Tracy could be happy.

"Oh my God," Julia blurted. "Tracy."

"What now?" Logan asked, turning off the ignition.

"We can't stay in different rooms. Everyone thinks we're a couple. You saw the way that guy at the front desk looked at us when we checked in. He thought it was weird, and it was, because we stayed in the same room last time. If anyone is likely to tip off the press about something out of the ordinary, it's the guy working the front desk."

The valet approached. They were about to lose what bit of privacy they had. Julia's mind was whirring. She'd been psyching herself up for holding hands at the wedding reception and ignoring her feelings while doing it, not preparing for a roommate.

"Pardon me if I find this weird coming from the person who just told me she didn't feel anything when she kissed me."

"And I'm also the person worried about her sister's wedding. The press comes back and I'm sunk. But I have no clue how we're supposed to explain this to the people at the front desk."

He rubbed the side of his face as if he couldn't possibly stand another minute of thinking about this. "Don't worry about it. I'll come up with something."

Easy enough for Logan to say. Right now, Julia

was worried about everything, especially the realization that she and Logan were about to share a room.

Logan turned the keys over to the valet and they went inside. The man with the familiar face was again manning the front desk.

"Yes. Hi," Logan started, clearly stalling. So much for coming up with something. "I need to check out of my room. I had a cold when we arrived, and I didn't want Ms. Keys to get sick when she's…"

Julia kicked Logan's foot. "He didn't want me to get sick right before my sister's wedding. It would be a disaster."

The desk clerk hesitated, looking back and forth between them, the moments ticking by at half speed. "Of course, Mr. Brandt. I'll send a bellman up to your room to move your belongings for you." He tapped away at his keyboard while Julia silently let out a sigh of relief.

"No need for that. I'll manage fine on my own."

"Let me know if you change your mind." The clerk swiped a room card. "And here's your extra key." The look he gave them said that he was in no way fooled, but Julia figured this guy had probably seen it all at this point.

They proceeded to the elevator. Today's second kiss seemed even more ill-advised now that she and Logan would be staying in the same room. Why did everything with Logan have to exist on such a slippery slope? She'd dipped her toes into those warm, inviting waters, and now it felt like she was up to her waist in trouble.

Logan went to collect his things while Julia quickly changed into pajama pants and a tank top. Apparently he was a light packer—he was opening her door minutes later, just as she was downing the second of the chocolates the maid had left on the pillows. She put her hands behind her back and crumpled the wrapper. Logan didn't need to know she wasn't just eating for two, she was eating chocolate for two.

"Hey, roomie," he quipped, flashing that beguiling smile of his and breezing into the room.

"Roomie is right. Platonic roommates. I don't want you getting any ideas." She discreetly dropped the evidence of her clandestine candy-eating into the trash.

"Getting ideas. You make me sound like a horny teenager. Don't worry about me. You made it pretty clear where you stand when you told me you didn't feel anything after our kiss." He wheeled his roller bag next to the bureau. "Which was a little odd considering how much you were actually participating in it."

"I plead hormonal insanity."

He toted his garment bag to the closet. "Where exactly do you expect me to hang my suit? You have enough clothes in here for a week."

"Oh, please. You're exaggerating." She walked over and began sliding hangers across the rod, cramming her clothes together. She took his suit from him and squeezed it in at the end.

"If it gets wrinkled, you're ironing it."

"Whatever it takes to appease you, Mr. Brandt."

She turned and he was right there, peering down at her breasts. "You have got to stop staring at my chest."

"I'm sorry, but when it's just the two of us, it's really hard not to look." A sly grin crossed his face, and he looped his finger in the direction of her chest. "They're spectacular. And it's hard not to think about the reason why they look like that. It's surprisingly sexy."

Julia's head was swimming. She hadn't been prepared for that. Did he really feel that way? Pregnancy had made her feel anything but sexy—tired and starving most of the time, although she had to admit that being around Logan had a way of helping her find her more alluring side. "Thank you. I just wish they didn't hurt so much."

"Hurt?" Logan traipsed across to the other side of his room and kicked off his shoes.

"Yes. They're sore. You blow more air into a balloon, it stretches. Same principle."

"You paint a lovely picture." He turned and began unbuttoning his pants. "You're totally taking the fun out of the idea of you with larger breasts, though."

Before she knew what was happening, he'd shucked his jeans and was folding them neatly. In black boxer briefs that showed off his long, lean legs, he was doing far too efficient a job of helping her feel sexy. Probably because she couldn't have him. He was forbidden fruit, the shiny apple she wasn't allowed to take a bite out of, no matter how tempting he was, all because she'd promised herself she wouldn't. And now Mr. Temptation was unbuttoning his shirt.

"Will you please go change in the bathroom?" she sputtered, clamping her eyes shut out of self-preservation.

"You can't be serious. I'm getting ready for bed. It's late and I'm wiped out. Drama makes me tired."

"So put on your pajamas already."

"These are my pajamas."

"You can't just sleep in your boxers. You have to put on something else." Every breath out of her was coming way too fast. Her heart was hammering.

"I didn't pack anything else. And it's not like you haven't seen me in way less than this."

Holy crap. His voice was so close. Much closer than it had been a moment ago. She sensed him moving closer. She could feel the warmth radiating from his body. She was too scared to open her eyes. She already knew how amazing he looked half-naked.

"If you aren't nice, I'll just sleep in the nude."

She wrestled with the threat—be mean and have him take his clothes off. Dangerous, but not the worst deal in the world. "Fine. I'll be nice."

"Then open your eyes. I promise you'll live through it."

Yeah, right. She opened her eyes all right, but just as quickly whipped around to avoid the sight of him. That meant she was now confronted with the image of a king-size expanse of luxury linens atop what she already knew was a very comfortable mattress.

Guilt ate at her, about a lot of things—bogarting the chocolate, not telling him the truth about the kiss and knowing she'd be in the bed while Logan was stuck on the couch. "I got the extra blanket out of the closet for you. You can take one of my pillows."

"What are you talking about? There are plenty of blankets." Logan pulled back the duvet, slipping under the covers. Well, his legs were blanketed. His stomach and chest weren't. No, those parts of him were too busy building their torment in her body. Judging by the way her body temperature was spiking, they'd built an entire torment city. He patted her side of the bed. "Doesn't the mom-to-be need to get some rest?"

"Oh, no. You're sleeping on the couch."

"No way. Have you seen how short that thing is? It wouldn't fit a guy who's six feet tall, and we both know I'm a lot taller than that."

This was not happening. She could see it now—in bed with Logan, fast asleep, somebody's hand wanders, somebody starts spooning, one body part finds another body part and the next thing they know, the baby-making parade is under way again. "Fine. Then I'll sleep on it."

He bolted upright in bed. "I'm not letting a pregnant woman sleep on that couch. Stop being ridiculous. We're capable of staying in the same bed and things not turning to…you know. Sex."

"Why would you think that? We've never slept in the same bed without it turning to sex. Ever."

"That can't be right."

She nodded and dared to step closer to the bed, even though she was being dogged by memories of the last time they were sharing a room in this hotel. Everything she saw—the bedside tables, the lamps and of course half-naked Logan—brought her back to that magical weekend. "Think about it. Never. Ever."

He reclined against the pillows, placing his hands behind his head. Good God, now it was like he was posing for the cover of a men's fitness magazine. And she had to act as if she wasn't fazed, even when her eyes were drawn to his well-defined chest, his abs, that narrow trail of dark hair beneath his belly button. Deep down, she was anything but ambivalent— she wanted to read every square inch of his body like she was studying braille. *Deep breaths. Enjoy the view. You're fine.*

Stupid straight and narrow. Of course she wasn't fine.

He pursed his lips and nodded slowly. "Huh. Maybe you're right. Well, first time for everything, right? Unless you'd rather fully immerse yourself in the role of my fake, serious girlfriend and seduce me." He rolled to his side and propped up his head with his hand.

"I have plenty of roles to play right now, thank you. Let's just get some sleep, okay? We have a long day ahead of us and I'm exhausted." She gingerly climbed beneath the covers. That one movement caused goose bumps to pepper her arms. Why her body had this unrelenting reaction to Logan was a mystery. She only knew it was a constant, and even after all the years of ups and downs, showed no sign of abating.

She flipped off the lamp, plunging them into darkness and quiet. She rolled to her side, away from him. He shifted in the bed, but he did what he always did, which was more of a flop than a gentle roll. She tried to ignore it. Tried to pay no attention to what her body was telling her, to snug herself up to him, let him envelop her in those arms, keep her warm, make her feel safe.

He shifted in the bed again, except this time she heard his slow and measured breaths. He'd dozed off already. He'd always been like that. His body seemed to have little trouble finding sleep.

She turned to her other side, which was far more comfortable. That put her close enough to touch him, to feel his soft breath against her face. It was hard not to continue to cling to an alternate version of what had happened after the reunion. Thoughts of what this moment might be like if things had been different, if he hadn't called things off. If they'd kept it together all summer. If he'd just believed that they belonged together. The same way she did, however much it pained her to acknowledge it.

Reaching over, she pulled the covers up over his arm. She'd always care for him. That wasn't going anywhere. She knew that much. And he might be the father of her child. That wasn't going anywhere, either. Her mind leaped ahead to the end of the weekend, to that moment when she would tell her parents. Maybe she should've had the DNA test. But then again, if she had, and the baby wasn't his, Logan would remove himself from her life forever.

She placed her hand on her lower belly. If she was being completely honest with herself, there were far too many moments when she really wished that

Logan was the dad. She wouldn't treat the baby any differently if he wasn't the father, but her heart really wanted it to be Logan. At least there had been love between them at some point. And despite their problems, they were friends. If there was a problem, she'd be able to call him, and she knew with certainty that he would help her. He would play the role of dad beautifully if that was what he became. As to the question of the role of husband and whether that day would come with her, the answer was no. She was too certain that friendship and attraction were not enough to sustain them. She needed him to love her.

Seven

"Ow! Ow!"

Logan opened one eye to darkness.

"Ow!" Jules yelped again. The bed shook.

He flipped on the lamp, wincing at the light, but alert. He hadn't really been asleep. Just dozing and replaying the kiss, along with her insistence that she'd felt nothing. "Are you okay? What's wrong?"

"Sorry. It's my leg. A cramp." She tossed back the covers and practically folded herself in half.

Scrambling out from under the comforter, he raced around to the other side of the bed. "Give me your leg." He grabbed her ankle, using both hands to flex her foot.

"Ow!" She reached for him, her face scrunched up in agony.

"Just lie back and try to relax." He gently raised her foot and planted it against his chest, massaging the calf muscle to unwind it from its painful contraction.

Julia knocked her head back on the bed and rocked it back and forth, a smile breaking across her face. "Oh, thank God. It's going away."

Logan pressed on her foot a little harder with his shoulder to get the full stretch while caressing her leg. Her skin was impossibly soft, conjuring so many pleasurable memories, accompanied right now by enticing visuals. Her pajama leg had slipped down to the middle of her thigh, revealing the part of her that he most loved wrapped around him. His hand spanned the back of her leg, rubbing from ankle to knee, up and down, the feel of her velvety skin slowly driving him mad, and yet there was no way he was about to let go. "Better?"

"Much. I keep getting charley horses in my sleep. It's a pregnancy thing. I'm sorry I woke you up."

"You didn't really. I was basically awake."

"I hope I wasn't snoring."

He laughed quietly. "You weren't. I was thinking about last night."

Several heartbeats of silence played out. "Last night?"

"The kiss. I don't want to give you a hard time about it, but am I crazy? Was there really nothing there?"

She chewed on her lower lip. Something of substance was running around in that beautiful head of hers, and he really hoped it wasn't the endless loop of denial. She sighed and looked him in the eye. "There was something there. There's always something there. Can't we leave it at that?"

Back and forth, he continued rubbing her leg. She was perfectly fine now. Her cramp was gone. He could walk away. Except that he couldn't, especially not after she'd finally told the truth. There in the soft, early-morning light, he couldn't get past how gorgeous she was. Rich brown hair splayed out against the white of the sheets, pleased grin on her face as she gave in to his touch, and then there were the sounds coming from her mouth. He kneaded her leg a little deeper with his fingers.

"That feels so good." Her voice was a sweet purr, uttering words he'd heard her say many times over their reunion weekend. She arched her back, then settled into the bed. Through the thin fabric of her tank top, he couldn't help but notice that her nipples had responded in a positive way. It took everything not to reach out and touch them. Not to lower himself to the bed and slip those skinny straps from her shoulders, cup her voluptuous breasts in his hands. Kiss her. Make her admit again that she felt something.

"Good. I'm glad. I like making you feel good." He couldn't have cared less that his words dripped with innuendo. All of the troubles and rough spots between them seemed so inconsequential right now. With the morning hours stretching out before them, all he wanted was to make love to her. He'd not only satisfy the thirst for her that never went away, he was certain that he'd know how she felt. He was tired of trying to interpret everything she said and did. The two rarely matched up.

With each pass of his hands, he made his journey a bit longer. He reached her slender ankle at the top of the pass, and now he was venturing beyond the back of her knee, lower and lower on her thigh.

"I could just stay like this all day." She put her hands behind her head and smiled. "My legs were killing me after all of that running around and standing all day yesterday."

"We don't need to be anywhere until your dress fitting, right?" That was at noon. He glanced at the clock, rubbing her leg, never losing contact. It was only a few minutes past seven. They had time. Oh boy did they have time. Everything in his body tensed at the idea, blood now fiercely coursing through him. Breathing became tougher, nearly forced. Thinking wasn't much easier. Would his way back in really be this simple?

"Yes. But don't talk about the wedding. It'll ruin the mood." She closed her eyes, her full mouth relaxed, a look of near-bliss on her face.

The mood. There was no mistaking that phrasing. He slowed the pace of his hand, dipping below her knee, inching lower along her thigh. All he could hear was his own heartbeat thumping in his ears and a breathy hum from Julia. He knew that hum, and it meant only one thing. His hand kept going, inches beyond previous passes. She didn't flinch. Her eyes remained closed. His body reacted with an abrupt stiffening in his chest, warmth creeping down his torso and below his waist, the most primal of responses to the beautiful creature in his clutches. Was this going to happen? Or was he still asleep, and stuck in a dream?

Whatever Julia could say about Logan and the ways in which he made her mad or hurt her, the man had amazing hands—one might go so far as to say he was gifted. And then there was his incredibly firm chest. With her foot planted against the muscular plane, she appreciated how solid it was.

His hands might have started as givers of therapeutic massage, but there was no mistaking their new role as tools of seduction. She had zero inclination to fight it. She didn't care to think about it. It was too good to be bad. Maybe this was what they needed to figure things out—work out their problems in bed.

He dipped his hand lower, his grip on the back of her leg just strong enough to tell her his intentions. Or at least what she surmised as his intentions. She begged the universe—please don't let this be another time when she'd managed to read him wrong. Her body was becoming far too accustomed to the idea of what could be coming next—Logan's sleeping attire on the floor, followed quickly by her own.

His thumb rode along the inside of her thigh, his other fingers clamped around the outside of her leg, his palm creating heat and friction. Slow and rhythmic, his movements brought about a trancelike state, one in which she didn't care about repercussions or what might happen to her stupid heart if she let Logan back in. She only knew that she wanted him in. Inside. Her.

She opened her eyes, one at a time, nervous she'd built this all in her head, and all she'd see was a disinterested Logan. Her truth-seeking brought a rich reward—his eyelids heavy with desire. How she loved seeing that expression on his face. It was the sexiest thing she could imagine. So sexy that she was sure there was no luckier woman anywhere on the planet right now. They were all alone. The door was locked. Clothes coming off and kissing and touching and lovemaking...they all felt possible now. She squirmed against the bed, goose bumps popping up along the surface of her skin. Her face flushed with dry heat, as if she were basking in the sun. Every inch of her wanted him.

"Have I mentioned how good that feels?" she asked, pleased with how genuinely seductive her voice was.

"It feels good to me, too." His gaze was so intent, eyes dark and focused on her, as if he had nothing on his mind but consuming her.

But he wasn't making a move, and now her brain was searching for the next thing to say. He hadn't left her with an opening. He hadn't led her to the next step. Perhaps he was waiting for her to take charge. Not surprising considering the way things had gone since Wednesday afternoon. She'd put him in his place more than once.

She wiggled her toes, then dug them into the skin of his chest. His hand was on one of the heavenly downward passes. He was mere inches from her center now. Her pajama pants were as bunched up around her upper thigh as they could be. If he wanted to go any farther, he'd have to slip his hand beneath the fabric.

"My pajamas are in the way." She held her breath, waiting for his response.

"I noticed. What do you want to do about that?"

The low rumble in his voice made her back arch again. He wanted her to say it. If she was going to repay the pleasure of the last few minutes, he deserved as much. "I want you to take them off."

His eyebrows bounced, conveying a cockiness he'd earned. "I'm a big fan of that answer." He gently lowered her leg until it was hanging off the edge of the bed like her other.

He towered over her as her vision drifted across his strong shoulders, down his muscled chest and defined stomach. Her eyes dipped lower, and she relished the thought of what would soon be hers, as there was no hiding his current enthusiasm—and readiness—for sex. His warm fingers curled under the waistband of her pajama pants, sending a shiver down her spine as he shimmied the fabric down her legs. She never wore panties under her pj's; it always felt like an unnecessary extra layer of clothes. Aside from her tank top, she was as bare to him as she could possibly be.

They hadn't marked this first moment of vulnerability when they first made love after the reunion. They were both too eager, all action, stopping for few words. At least the first time. There was a stillness to this moment, an anticipation that left her breathless. Perhaps it was because this time they'd arrived by chance, the two of them falling together, as was their natural inclination.

He stepped out of his boxers and she had to shift up onto her elbows to admire him, all chiseled physique and masculinity. A sly smile crossed his heavenly lips as he stretched out on the bed next to her. He cupped her face and kissed her softly, gently. He took his time. She loved that about sex with Logan. He rarely rushed, and she was always the priority, even when they were both feeling frantic. His tongue wound in languid circles with hers, enough to make her feel dizzy. Their two kisses yesterday had taken hours to shake off. She'd be lucky if she could stand up straight anytime soon after this one.

He flattened his hand against her belly and slipped it underneath her top. She sat up for a second and removed it, then settled next to him again. His hand slowly crept to the flat plane in the center of her chest, fingers smoothing up over the top of one breast; blood rushed to flood her skin, tightening her nipple.

"I don't want to hurt you. You'll have to tell me what's too much." He gently circled the hardened peak with the tip of his finger, teasing and making her crazy in the process.

"It all feels good right now. All of it." She watched as he lowered his head and gave her nipple a soft lick, swirling his tongue around it before drawing it into his mouth. She closed her eyes and reached down be-

tween them, wrapping her fingers around his steely
length and stroking.

A low groan left his throat and his mouth returned
to hers, kissing her with greater vigor than before.
He rolled to his back and pulled her with him, inviting her to press her full body weight into his. They
fell into a kiss both soft and intense, different from
the other kisses this weekend. There was a freeness
that hadn't been there before—probably the feeling
of setting aside her reservations. She rocked her body
against his, craving deeper contact, everything between her legs hungry for him.

Luckily, no birth control was necessary. She strad-
dled his hips, not giving up on their mind-blowing
kiss, their tongues winding in circles as the scruff
on his face faintly scratched at her cheeks and chin.
He had the most amazing smell in the morning—the
faintest traces of woodsy cologne, blended with sleep.
It was intoxicating and all his own. She raised her
bottom and took his erection in hand, guiding him
inside her. Her eyes drifted closed as he filled her perfectly, inch by inch. The sense that she'd reached the
promised land was immense, probably because she
remembered exactly how good this would be, but it
was an odd sensation—her body immersed in quiet
jubilation and eager anticipation at the same time.

He took her breasts into his hands, squeezing, then
raising his head and sucking on each nipple. The tension inside her had been quickly building already,
but that sent her racing for her peak. She kissed him
again, wanting to languish in this beautiful moment,

knowing that whatever happened this weekend, she would at least have another beautiful memory to stow away in her head. He slipped his hand between their bodies, his thumb finding her apex. He wound it in tiny circles, knowing exactly how to play this, and she luckily could dictate the pressure with her body weight. Still, it was as if he'd been born with the instruction manual for her body inside his head, and he pursued a tempo that perfectly matched the rhythm of his thrusts.

His breaths came shorter now, much like hers, and the muscles of his torso and hips began to coil tighter beneath her. The peak was upon her, her breath hitching in her chest, and everything around her was falling away…everything except Logan. The waves kept coming, and then he cried out with a forceful thrust, his arms reining her in tightly. She collapsed against him as contentment enveloped her. She was exactly where she'd wanted to be from the moment she first saw him two days ago—safe in his embrace.

Logan didn't hesitate to pull her back into their kiss, the motions of his lips helping her savor this blissful moment.

Then Logan's cell phone rang.

It registered as a minor annoyance with Julia, but he ended the kiss, rolling away from her. "No no no," he groaned.

She smiled and smoothed her hand over his stomach. She wasn't about to let technology cut this short. "Let it go to voice mail. We have all morning." She drew a lazy circle in the center of his chest with her finger. "Now where were we?"

He closed his eyes and moved her hand. "I hate to say this, but we're done for the morning." The phone continued its interruption. "That ringtone is literally the only sound that can ruin the mood." He rolled away again and strode across the room.

"Just ignore it. Come back." She patted the mattress, wishing she could transport him back to where he'd just been.

"It's my mom. I have to answer it. She'll just keep calling if I don't. Plus, the mere thought of my mom makes a repeat performance impossible."

Julia sighed and scooted back on the bed, resting her head on the pillow. She pulled the sheet up to her chin. The moment was indeed over.

"Mom, hey, I'm sorry I haven't called. Things have been crazy busy since I got here." He cradled the phone between his ear and shoulder, pulling a pair of basketball shorts out of his suitcase and tugging them on.

And there went my view.

"Oh. Yeah. Right. Jules and me. We should probably talk about that." He shook his head and looked down at the floor. "I know. You're right. I'm sorry you had to find out from the news."

Oh crap. Right there was proof that Logan had put little thought into his plan. Of course his mom would find out about it. She not only lived in town, she was as connected as could be—lifelong resident and a district court judge. The rumor mill had probably started churning the instant Logan told his tale to the reporters. It was a miracle she hadn't called him last night.

"I know. I know." He nodded eagerly. "Hey, Mom, let me put you on speaker for a second." He pressed a button on his phone and placed it on the bureau, then threw a T-shirt over his head and threaded his arms into it.

Logan's mother's voice rang out over the speaker. "I know you're busy with the wedding, but I'd like to see the two of you together before tomorrow. Otherwise I might not get any time alone with you at all."

He closed his eyes, kneading his forehead, clearly wrestling with the conversation. Difficult to explain or not, they were going to have to come clean with his mom as well. "Don't you need to be in court today?"

"As luck would have it, there's a gas leak at the courthouse. I swear it's something new every day. They really need to put some money into that building. Normally I'd complain, but if it means I get to see my handsome son and the girlfriend I'd always hoped he'd find a way to be with, I'm happy. So, no, court is not in session today."

Eight

The press had stayed away. Logan was able to retrieve the car from the valet like a civilized person— no more sneaking around. Whatever his fabrication had done to annoy Julia or infuriate Tracy, it had been worth it. Now he just had to find out how much it would irritate his mother when she, too, learned it was a lie. *Great.*

Only after what had transpired with Julia that morning, he wasn't entirely sure it was a lie. They hadn't had a conversation about it. During his time on the phone with his mom, Julia had received a call from Tracy. He'd hopped in the shower while she talked about lunch plans with her sister, then it had been Julia's turn to commandeer the bathroom. Room service arrived with breakfast; he got a few texts from

Carter about the two of them picking up the rings.
Julia bustled around the hotel room, Logan did much
of the same, and it all just went back to the way it had
been twenty-four hours ago. Except now there was
sex with Julia fresh in his mind, and he couldn't stop
thinking about the surreality of that moment when it
was clear she wanted him.

Was Julia experimenting? Was she trying to sound
him out? Was she finally coming around to his way
of thinking? That they should figure out a way to forgive each other and move forward? He wasn't about
to see his child go without a father, no matter how
much he worried that Julia might not be capable of
loving him, at least not forever.

Unfortunately, Julia was on the phone with her
Aunt Judy for the duration of the drive to Logan's
mom's. Meaning, yet again, no conversation or clarification. The wedding had taken center stage. And
there wasn't a damn thing Logan could do about it.

When they arrived at the house, Logan took Julia
in through the side door that led to the kitchen. The
room never changed—simple white tile countertops,
checkerboard dish towel draped over the oven handle, a ceramic cookie jar shaped like a cupcake, and
the picture window above the sink, overlooking the
backyard. Coffee was on, also no surprise. His mom
was an all-day-long coffee drinker, just as his dad had
been. He couldn't imagine his childhood home without it. And that one particular aroma brought back
more than memories, good and bad; it transported

him to a time when he was a different person, a kid trying to figure out how to be a man.

As much as he loved this house, he never stayed here when he came back into town. Sleeping in his old bed would've invited too much introspection, along with a sore back. Luckily, his mom had converted his room into a sewing and craft space, and the one his brothers had shared still housed their old bunk beds. His mom didn't seem eager to nudge time ahead, and he'd be the last person to push.

His mother waltzed into the kitchen, her chin-length curly dark hair tied back with a colorful scarf. Even with a day off from work, she was the epitome of put-together. Jewelry. Makeup. "I should've known you'd come in through the side door." She beamed as they beelined for each other, arms wide open.

"It just feels weird to go to the front. The mail-man and strangers go to the front door." They embraced, both holding on tight. Hugs from his mom always lasted a heartbeat longer than most, a powerful reminder of how much they'd needed each other after his father's death. She'd lost her best friend and husband of fifteen years. Logan and his brothers had lost their hero, mentor and coach. If any family had ever held each other up, they had.

"And here's the lovely Julia." His mother hadn't let go of his shoulders, but she was now looking back and forth between them, a prideful smile on her face. "I always wondered if you two would find a way."

Logan's stomach wobbled at the tone in his mother's voice. It was different from Julia's parents. They were always full of sunny optimism. His mom was an upbeat person, but she also had an unflinching critical eye. She could pick apart any charade. Could she see what was lying beneath the surface between them? That they were drawn to each other, however messed up things happened to get? Or was his mom hinting that she knew what was going on and was simply waiting for him to come out with it?

"Mrs. B. You look amazing. As always." Julia stepped closer, and that was enough to coax his mother from his arms.

"Coming from one of the most beautiful women in the world, I'll take that compliment any day."

He stood back and admired the two of them. Even his mom and Julia looked right together.

"It's all smoke and mirrors, you know," Julia said. "They put me in so much makeup for my movies and photo shoots, it's ridiculous. You have me beat with those high cheekbones."

"Well, thank you. Flattery will get you everywhere." Logan's mom draped her arm across Julia's shoulders. "Can I get you two some coffee? Followed by an explanation of what in the world is going on that I find out from the newspaper that you're a couple after all this time?"

There was his cue to come out with it. "Mom, I had to say that to get the press to go away. To make them stop asking Julia about her costar."

She nodded as if the news was no surprise. "I see. Well, that's a disappointment, but I thought it seemed a little out of the blue." She directed her gaze at Julia. "Coffee?"

His mom pulled two mugs from the cabinet, but Julia had cut way back on coffee because of the pregnancy.

"Oh, no, Mrs. B. I'm good. I had plenty at the hotel. In fact, may I use your powder room?"

"Of course. You know where it is." Logan's mom filled a fresh cup for Logan and topped off her own mug as Julia left to go to the bathroom.

"So?" his mom asked, leaning back against the counter and arching her eyebrows at him. "Anything else you want to share with me?"

There it was—the only invitation she'd extend for him to apologize. "I'm sorry you had to hear the story from the news. It's just complicated. Like most things with Jules."

His mother shook her head. "That's not what I was asking. How far along is she?"

Logan nearly choked on his coffee. "What?"

"One of the most successful actresses in Hollywood is getting a little thick in the middle? I don't think so. And she's glowing. Good God, if ever a woman glowed, it's her." She sipped from her mug. "Declining the coffee was the final clue. Julia has never turned down a cup of my coffee. Ever. I spent an awful lot of years as a prosecutor. I'm good at figuring things out."

I'll be damned. Logan leaned back and peered through the doorway into the hall. "She's three months along. But it's a secret. Nobody knows." The rest was sitting on his lips. He wasn't keen on saying any of it, but his mother was likely one or two pointed questions away from figuring everything out. He cleared his throat, then came clean—the reunion, the phone call. And the worst of it—her ex.

His mother took another sip of coffee. "So you're telling me there's a chance I'm about to become a grandmother, but you aren't together. Do you love her?"

Just then, Julia ducked into the room. "I didn't want y'all to think I got lost. My sister called and I need to call her back. I'll just be in the living room if that's okay."

"Of course. Feel free to use my office if you need it," his mother replied.

Julia retreated to the other room. Logan was still mulling over his mother's question.

"Well? Do you?" she asked.

He knew the answer, but he wished he didn't have to qualify it. "I do, on some level, but it's not as simple as that. If the baby is mine, we have to get married. I don't see any other way it's going to work. I have to accept my responsibility."

"Of course you do. You've always stepped in and done what was right. You did that when your father passed."

"See? Exactly. Similar situation, but Julia doesn't agree. There comes a time when things happen and you just have to man up and do your job. But she doesn't see my point. If she'd listen to me and get a paternity test, it would make this much more clear-cut."

His mother shook her head in slow motion, as if she wanted him to feel every bit of condemnation that was coming from her expression. "Please tell me you haven't actually said that to her."

"It's a legitimate request. Any man in the world would ask the question."

"Of course they would, but that doesn't mean I don't expect my son to see the problem. A paternity test does nothing more than give you a free pass to walk away if the answer is that you're not the father, and makes you beholden to her if you are."

"I'm not looking for a free pass. That's not what this is about. But I don't know how I'm supposed to make a decision without that information."

His mother cocked both eyebrows, her lips pursed. She clunked her coffee cup in the porcelain sink. "Logan Brandt, I thought I raised you better than that. How do you think Julia feels?" She then proceeded to say virtually everything Julia had said to him about living with complete uncertainty, all on her own. "Not only that, but her career is on the line here. She's going to have to take time off from films, quite possibly raise a child on her own. It's not easy, Logan. I'm speaking from experience. I had to be a single mom after your dad passed away. Trying to work my way through the prosecutor's office and raise three boys? It was hard."

"I know, Mom. I do. I was there for the whole thing, remember? I did my best to step up to the plate then, too. I'm not going to walk away from her if the baby is mine."

"And I'm telling you right now that if I was Julia, that would not be my misgiving. I'd be far more worried about what you'll do if the baby isn't yours. It would be difficult for any man to step into that role with another man's child. But take your history with her and it's got to be twice as hard. She has prepared herself for you to walk away. Again. That's why she was not particularly enamored of your line about accepting responsibility."

He stared down at the kitchen floor, realizing how much Julia had let her guard down that morning when they'd made love. How would he and Julia ever get past this? It was a catch-22 unlike any he'd ever experienced. "I just don't know what to do anymore. I only want to do what's right, but I feel like I'm damned if I do and damned if I don't."

"It's not just up to you. You both have to arrive at the same decision. That's the only way you both end up happy."

"That's the exact thing we're horrible at."

"What did your daddy always say when he was helping you with your pitching? He told you that practice makes perfect. You have to keep trying."

He kneaded his forehead. Everything going through his mind was starting to give him a headache. "Honestly, I'm not even sure what to try with Julia anymore."

"Something tells me you'll figure it out." She reached out and clasped her hand over his. "Hold on one minute. I want to run upstairs and get you something."

Logan poured out the last of his coffee and rinsed the sink. His mother always kept a spotless kitchen. He stood and looked out at the backyard, exactly the spot where his father had played catcher while Logan perfected his pitch. The mound they'd built with load after load of dirt from the back of the lot was barely visible now, covered in grass and mostly sunken in with the rest of the lawn. Still, the traces remained. Just as the traces of his father remained in his head—James Brandt's proud stance, kind ways and deep voice, which became rough and grumbly as the cancer slowly took him away. Logan could still hear his dad's words—not his final utterance to his son, but the one that made the deepest impression, echoing for years, never shared with anyone until Julia. *You have to be the man of the house now, son. Take care of your mom and your brothers. I can't be here to do it.*

Talk about life's patterns repeating—he had to take care of Julia and the baby. Something deep inside him told him it was the only way. But would Julia let him? And would she want him to stay?

Logan jumped when his mom pressed her hand to his back.

"Logan, hon. You okay?"

He nodded and turned, choking back those memories of his dad. "Yeah. Of course."

She held out a small gray felt drawstring pouch. "This is what I went to get."

Logan was in shock. The last thing he'd expected

her to give him today was his grandmother's ring. He'd been told from a young age that he would get it whenever it came time to propose to a woman. He hadn't even asked for the ring with his previous engagement, the one eventually broken, to a woman he'd never bothered to bring home. He'd made every excuse in the book, but the truth was that he'd known his mother would see right through the facade. What he'd had with his former fiancée wasn't real. "Mom. Really?"

She nodded and opened the pouch, revealing the large pale pink diamond in the center, surrounded by white diamonds, all set in platinum. "Yes, really. I have a feeling you're going to need this in the coming days or weeks, or maybe hours. Hard to tell with you two. I don't want you to be unprepared. She'll take you more seriously with a ring." She pulled it from its resting place, turning it in her fingers. "I always forget how beautiful it is. It will look perfect on her hand."

Julia's voice filtered in from the hall. "Okay, Trace. I'll see you in thirty at the boutique."

Logan's mom dropped the ring back into the tiny bag, yanked the drawstring and folded it into his hand. He shoved it into his pocket, still disbelieving that his mother had given it to him, all while wrestling with what would have to happen for Julia to accept it from him.

Julia wandered into the kitchen and tucked her phone into her purse. "It's a modern miracle. My sister doesn't hate me today. Or at least not as much as yesterday."

Logan's mom nodded and stepped closer to Julia, eyeing her belly. He watched in horror as the look on her face changed, as if she was turning into a grandmother before his eyes. "Don't worry, hon. She won't hate you at all once she finds out your little secret."

Julia smiled politely and waved at Logan's mom as they said their goodbyes, but she could only sustain her pleasantness until the side door was closed and Mrs. Brandt was out of earshot. "I can't believe you told her." She should have waited until Sunday to tell Logan. She never should've given in to that little voice inside that said he deserved to know as soon as she'd had her first chance.

"I didn't have to tell her. She guessed."

"What?" Julia stopped at the bottom of the driveway. "How could she guess that I'm pregnant?"

Logan grabbed her hand and pulled her toward the car. "Come on. Let's not have this discussion in the middle of the street. You're worried about keeping your secret, all we need is for some hapless dog walker to wander by and overhear you."

"Okay. Fine," Julia grumbled and got into the car. "I don't understand how she possibly could've guessed."

Logan wasted little time driving away from the curb. "I'm telling you right now, there's no way you make it through this wedding without everyone figuring it out. The clues are there. Your chest is bigger. You pass up coffee. You're glowing."

"Glowing is such baloney." Julia dismissed the comment with a flip of her hand.

"What? You *are* glowing. I probably could've figured out what was going on if I hadn't been so busy thinking about how hot you look right now."

Heat rushed to her cheeks. Logan and his compliments—so disarming in an argument. "That's not fair. You're flirting so I won't give you a hard time."

"Nope. Just being honest. The only way I can get to you is with total honesty."

She sat back in her seat and wrapped her arms around her waist. Her plan was starting to feel more and more stupid, only it was too late to veer off course. "Thank you. That was nice of you to say."

"If we're being honest, I want to know what happened this morning."

She nearly laughed. "You know what happened. You were there. And I'm pretty sure you enjoyed it."

"That's not what I mean." He quickly cut onto a side street. He put the gearshift into Park beneath the shade of a looming oak tree. "I need to know what's going on. What you're thinking. Last night you insisted you felt nothing when I kissed you and then this morning you change your story. I need to know what you're thinking."

If Logan wanted the truth about her feelings, it would take several hours to unravel it. They were messy. And complicated. And ever-changing. She glanced at the digital clock on the dash. "I'm thinking that if you don't get me to my dress fitting in the next fifteen minutes, my sister is going to blow a gasket."

"I really don't care. I'll deal with your sister if I have to, and I'm tired of the wedding putting everything else on hold. Not talking about this isn't going to help us navigate the maze ahead of us."

She sucked in a deep breath. Dealing with the wedding was a pain, but at least it had afforded her a few moments where she could stop worrying about what the future held. Her mind drifted to those heavenly moments just a few hours ago, when nothing else mattered but the two of them, perfectly in sync. "I wanted you this morning. You touch me and all I want is to give in. And it was wonderful. But that just makes everything more depressing."

Logan blinked in disbelief. "I'm not sure what about that was depressing."

The frustration was building inside her again. "I hate that we can only get our act together in bed. That doesn't feel great."

He sighed, tugging the keys out of the ignition and tossing them down into the cup holder. Apparently they were going to be there for a while. "We do have that problem, don't we?"

She'd been bracing for an argument from him. Instead, he agreed, which felt far worse. "So I don't know where we are, other than at an impasse."

"An impasse with benefits. That's a new one."

"Very funny. You know, even if I forgive you for dumping me after the reunion, that doesn't change the fact that you did it. That's the thing I can't get past right now."

"I said I was sorry. You're the one who doesn't want to accept my apology."

"It's not about that. It's not about saying that you're sorry." *It's that you don't love me. And I can't make you do it.* She blew out a breath, and the quiet felt like it might suffocate her. There were no words she could say aloud to erase the empty feeling he'd left her with the day he took his love—or at least the promise of his love—away.

"Then what is it about?" He turned and reached for her hand, enveloping it in his. "Talk to me. Tell me whatever it is you need to say so we can get past this."

How did she even put this into words? She looked up at him, fighting tears. It felt as though she was about to scratch open her own wounds. "You have to understand, I was so happy when I flew home to California that day after the reunion. I was so thankful that the planets had finally aligned and we were on the same page."

He nodded. "I know. I felt that way, too."

"And then you called and left me a message." She shook her head and closed her eyes, praying for strength. "I remember it so clearly, too. I'd gone outside to get the mail and my phone was inside on the coffee table. You have no idea how my heart leaped when I came inside and saw that you'd called." Just telling the story was making her heart feel impossibly heavy, as if it might fold in on itself from the weight of the past. "And then you told me that I was wrong.

That we wouldn't work. That our weekend had been fun, but we had to admit it was over. It felt worse than having the rug pulled out from under me. It felt like the earth had disappeared. One minute I saw a future for us and the next minute it went away. Poof. Disappeared."

"I'm sorry I hurt you. I don't know what else to say. I can't undo what I did."

"And then we talk in your hotel room the other night and you tell me that this all started because of the Derek thing. It's so stupid."

Logan sucked in a deep breath. "It's not just that."

She waited for him to say something else, but he didn't. "Then what?"

"I was a mess walking into that reunion. Feeling sorry for myself, depressed about my job. And that's the one time, out of all of the reunions that we've seen each other at, that you decide you want to be with me? You didn't want me. You just wanted another project."

She narrowed her stare at him. "I don't even know what that means."

"You're always trying to fix guys. They always have some tragic fault that you seem to think you can fix. And it usually just bites you in the butt at the end. Either that or you actually accomplish what you set out to do and then you're looking for the next person to save. And frankly, I don't care to belong in either of those camps."

"That's so untrue." She crossed her arms and stared out the windshield. Or was that true? Was that really her pattern?

"Just think about it, Jules. When we first started going out, I was a project, wasn't I?"

"That's not the reason I liked you. That's not the reason I wanted to go out with you. I thought you were cute and I couldn't believe that you would even pay attention to me, let alone like me."

"But once you got to know me, you realized just how lost I was. I needed your help. And you did help me. I will always be grateful for that. But once you were sure I'd be fine on my own, you dumped me. I wasn't about to go through that with you again."

Oh. That. All these years later and they'd never, ever, talked about their first breakup. Never.

"I don't want to dredge up the past," he continued. "But it hurt a lot."

"We were kids. Did it really mean that much to you?"

Disbelief and disappointment crossed his face. Julia wasn't sure which one hurt more. "I don't know, Jules. We were in love, weren't we? Did we mean that much to you?"

She nearly choked on the answer. "Of course we meant that much. Of course we did." She stared down at her hands in her lap. "But I thought it was inevitable. You were going off to UCLA, destined to be the famous baseball player. You were going to have every girl in the world you ever wanted. I couldn't compete with that."

He shrugged. "Fair enough. I get that. Maybe we wouldn't have been able to make it work. Very few people do. But it doesn't change the fact that everything bad between us started right then."

They were both quiet, Julia trying to absorb just how badly she'd hurt him. Did it all even out? Was that the way love was supposed to work? "Just so you know, you were not a project. I've never, ever thought of you that way. Not when we were seventeen and not three months ago. You have to believe me when I say that. I just wanted to help you." *Because I love you.* The words were right there, but she couldn't say them. They would go unreturned, and nothing would be more painful than that.

He nodded, but didn't seem entirely convinced. "Okay. That's good to know."

"You know, you said that there was no telling how things would've played out the first time, but can you really say that about this summer, too? What if we'd done well? What if we'd worked it all out? What then? Just think of how different this weekend could be. We wouldn't have to be sitting here wondering what the future held."

Except that the question of paternity would still be hanging over their heads. They might be together, they might even still be in love, but if she'd had the test and taken away the uncertainty, there was a chance that in itself would've been the end.

"Look, I'm sorry if I misread the situation," he said. "I'm sorry that I hurt your feelings. But you have to understand that I did what felt right at the time. It wasn't pleasant for me, either. The summer was hard. I missed you a lot."

"You did?" She looked up at him. Funny how that one tiny admission softened her heart. "Why didn't you call me? I would've talked to you."

"I could ask you the same thing, since you found out you were pregnant with what might be my child."

Well then. The phone *did* work both ways. "Yeah. I see your point."

"So now what?"

Facing him, she scanned his handsome features, wondering if he felt better about any of this. She was still processing. "I don't know. I don't know what to think anymore."

"Okay. Well, let me ask you this. What do you want from me? Let's not even put the question of the baby in the mix. As a man, what do you want from me?"

Talk about a loaded question. It was hard to separate the baby from the equation, but he'd asked her to. That meant she could only go to one place for the answer—the way she'd felt after he'd broken up with her, before she'd found out she was pregnant. "I want you to love me." It was as much a plea to the universe as it was a request of Logan.

"I'll always love you, Jules. There will always be love between us. And you know, I could ask the same of you. I would love it if you could find a way to love me. For real. For the long haul. I realize you were hurt, but you didn't call me when you found out you were pregnant. That doesn't really feel like love."

She felt as if the air had been squeezed out of her. She'd spent an entire summer cursing Logan's existence and a month wishing she didn't have to tell him about the pregnancy. Then she'd spent the last two days thinking he was being nothing but a selfish jerk about the baby. Now who'd been the selfish jerk? She was pretty sure it was her. "You're right and I'm so sorry. That was wrong." *Really, really wrong.* "So now what?"

"Kiss and make up?"

"Yeah, I guess it's time for us to forgive each other. It's not like we don't have other problems to deal with."

"Okay. I forgive you. But they don't just call it kiss and make up. We make up, we kiss."

She dropped her head and hoped to convey admonishment with a single look.

"Think of it as a fact-finding mission. We're both trying to figure out how we feel right now, and we both admit this is the part we always get right. And honestly, I feel like I break through some of your stubbornness every time I kiss you."

"I'm not that stubborn."

"Now you're being stubborn about being stubborn."

Before she could say another word, he clasped the back of her neck and pulled her mouth to his. She insisted on a few seconds of hesitation, but gave in to it quickly, tilting her head as he opened his lips and sent that familiar tingle right through her. She pressed into him. He pushed right back. *Hello, slippery slope.*

She pulled back, her mind buzzing, but he held her head close, their foreheads pressed together, noses touching, both of them breathing heavily. "Logan, we can't. You're going to get me all riled up again. And I'm going to be late."

He blew out an exasperated breath. "Yes. Of course. God forbid we disappoint the bride."

Nine

Julia opened the door for Belle's Bridal Boutique to one of the most unfunny pieces of music she could imagine right now. Electronic chimes played "Here Comes the Bride," announcing her arrival. *Ding ding ding-ding. Here comes the bride. Ha ha ha.*

The woman working behind a tall counter near the entrance looked up and gasped. "Your sister said you would be coming." She hurried out from behind her post and thrust out her hand. "I'm Tiffany. I'm the manager. I told myself I wouldn't get too excited, but I can't believe you're in our little shop."

Julia smiled and nodded. "Well, your little shop is just darling." Her eyes glazed over at the racks of white dresses surrounding them. It was hard to imagine she would ever find herself in this situation of her own accord—picking out a wedding gown. That would mean she'd not only managed to find the right guy, she'd managed to hold on to him, and the entire world knew she was incapable of that.

Her father, sitting in the center of the showroom in a fussy white upholstered armchair, waved her over. He'd been stationed in an area with a carpeted pedestal and three-way mirror. "Hey, Junebug. Where's Mr. Baseball?"

"He went with Carter to pick up the wedding bands. He'll be back in about a half hour." Julia plopped herself down on a love seat, thoughts of her talk with Logan still tumbling around in her head. He'd asked how she felt, but he hadn't offered his own take on much of anything beyond their painful past. She wasn't ready to slap a label on anything, but that kiss had sure given her something to chew on.

"Your mother is in the back with Tracy and the tailor. They should be out any minute."

"Can I get you something to drink?" Tiffany asked. "Your mother and sister are enjoying a glass of champagne."

Not for me. "Water would be wonderful."

"I'll be right back. Surely you remember Ms. Sully from your first fitting." Tiffany's drawl was so thick that the seamstress's name came out as one word—*Mssully.* "She'll bring out your dress as soon as she finishes up with your sister."

Right on cue, a billowing white skirt peeked out from behind the expanse of mirrors. Tracy floated into view. Julia didn't even have a second to process the vision before the tears started. She loved her sister to the very depths of her heart, even when Tracy was being a pain in her backside. Seeing her in a stunning off-the-shoulder gown that would've made Cinderella jealous enough to spit, all she could do was cry. Her mother wasn't doing much better, hand held to her mouth, shaking her head, a blubbering mess.

Julia rose from her seat and went to Tracy as she stepped up onto the platform. "You are the most gorgeous bride I have seen in my entire life."

Tracy gleamed into the mirror, turning side to side and smoothing the dress. She looked down at Julia with pure elation on her face. "Thank you so much. I can't believe this is finally happening." This was what Julia had hoped for this weekend—her sister, blissful and basking in the glory of being the bride. "And honestly, I can't believe that something is actually going right for once. As soon as you got here the other day, I was sure this wedding was going to be a disaster."

And just like that, Julia was thunked back down to earth.

"I really don't think the dress needs any more alterations, Trace," their mother said. "It's perfect. Absolutely perfect."

"I agree." Ms. Sully added as she filed out from behind the mirror with a pincushion on her wrist and a pink measuring tape around her neck. "Now let's get your sister into her dress. This should be quick. It was close to perfect for the first fitting, but I do want to check the length."

Tiffany sidled out from the back room and handed Julia a bottle of water.

"No champagne, Jules?" Tracy asked. "We're celebrating."

She'd worried about this, especially after Logan had made the comment about the secret being impossible to keep. Julia rarely passed up a glass of bubbly, especially not celebratory. "I have a bit of a headache." Not entirely a lie. The summit with Logan in the car had given her more than her head could handle.

"Maybe it'll loosen you up," Tracy countered.

"I'm good." Julia hoped like heck her sister would just drop it.

"Your fitting room is right over here," Tiffany said, thankfully taking the focus off what Julia was and was not willing to drink.

Ms. Sully followed as Tiffany directed Julia to a small room with an upholstered bench. Next to a standing mirror hung Julia's dress, the one she'd tried on the last time she'd been in town. It was pretty, albeit maybe not what Julia would've picked out— pale pink organza with a strapless bodice and puffy skirt—so fluffy that Julia had commented that if the dress were yellow, she'd look like a lemon meringue pie. Tracy had not found that funny.

Julia's mother joined them, closing the door behind her. "The bridesmaids' dresses are so lovely."

"Everyone else had their final fittings weeks ago," Ms. Sully said, unzipping the dress, taking it from its hanger and handing it to Julia. "I would've preferred to have done the same for you."

Julia slipped out of her sundress and into the gown. "I'm sorry. My schedule has been crazy." Stepping in front of the mirror, she tugged up the dress to her armpits, holding it to her chest.

Ms. Sully took the zipper in hand, but judging by the sound of it, and the way the dress had not snugged up around Julia, she didn't get more than a few inches. "It's too small in the bust."

Julia's mother tittered. "That can't be right. The Keys women are blessed with childbearing hips and that's about it. We did not get much in the boob department."

"Look for yourself." Ms. Sully struggled to pull the back of the dress closed, cutting off Julia's oxygen supply in the process.

Julia felt the blood drain from her face. *Oh no no no no no.* She hadn't accounted for this. She'd tried the dress on with a padded bra the first time—a very padded bra. The one she was wearing right now had only a thin lining. She'd been sure that would be enough difference to accommodate her expanded endowments. Apparently not.

Julia's mom let out a snort of frustration. "This doesn't make any sense. I was here when you tried it on the first time. Are you sure this is the same dress? Did you grab one of the other bridesmaids' dresses?"

"The other girls have all taken their dresses home. This is the last one."

A knock came at the door and Tracy walked in,

back in her preppy fuchsia-and-lime-green sheath dress, bottle of champagne and three glasses in hand. "I brought the party and I'm not taking a no from Jules this time." The smile on her face didn't last long when she saw the back of Julia's dress.

"Oh no, Jules. What did you do?"

"Me? Why do you immediately blame me?"

Tracy set the bottle down on a small table and hurried over, elbowing Ms. Sully out of the way and yanking on the back of the dress. "Suck it in. Come on." She grunted and tugged, but it wouldn't budge. "What on earth have you been eating?"

"It's not her waist, although that's definitely tighter, too. It's her bust. Her chest is too large for the dress." Ms. Sully pulled the tape measure from around her neck.

Tracy rounded out from behind Julia, confronting her head-on and staring at her bust. "You got a boob job and didn't tell me?" She poked her right in the chest.

"Ow." Julia winced.

Tracy's eyes grew wide. "Oh my God. You *did* get a boob job. Before my wedding? Now you're trying to steal my thunder by having bigger boobs?"

"I did not get a boob job." Julia wished she would've thought about that answer for even two seconds. That would've given her an out. But it would've been a lie, one that would eventually come to light.

"The only other thing that could make this dramatic a difference is pregnancy," Ms. Sully said nonchalantly, as if she were telling everyone that it might rain next week.

Tracy's eyes practically popped out of her head. "No."

"Pregnant?" Their mother let out a whimper. Julia wasn't sure she'd ever heard a sadder sound.

"Oh. My. God." Tracy's face turned that shade of red again. This was getting to be far too common a sight. "That's why you won't drink any champagne. I *knew* something was up."

Julia's heart was about to pound its way out of her chest, but she wasn't going to deny something she'd have to come clean about in two days. Plus, she was tired. Flat-out exhausted. "Yes, I'm pregnant. I didn't want anyone to know until after the wedding was over. The spotlight is supposed to be Tracy's right now."

Tracy shook her head, practically boring a hole through Julia with her piercing eyes. Her jaw was so tight, it was making the veins in her neck stick out. "You really are trying to ruin my wedding. You knew this was going to happen. You knew your dress wouldn't fit." She turned, poured herself a glass of champagne, and downed it.

"I had no idea it wouldn't fit. I didn't think it was going to be that big of a difference."

"And you just had to orchestrate this to suck the air out of my happiness, didn't you? Right after I'd tried on my dress and we'd all cried together and had such a beautiful moment. The big famous actress had to go for maximum drama." Her voice was ice cold.

Their mother was apparently still catching up. "A baby? I'm going to be a grandmother? Who's the father? Please don't tell me it's that terrible Derek."

"Mom. It's not Derek." At least she had one answer she could give without hesitation.

Ms. Sully leaned over Julia's shoulder. "I've got the measurements I need. I'll do my best to let it out before tomorrow, but no promises. Bring me the dress when you've changed your clothes. I need to get right to work."

Julia grasped the woman's arm. "I'm begging you. Please don't say anything to anyone about this."

"Of course, dear. You can count on my discretion."

"I'm out of here. I can't deal with this." But Tracy wasn't *really* out of there, because she got back in Julia's face. "You make me wish I hadn't made you my maid of honor. I just want you to think about that." A single tear rolled down her cheek, which felt like a knife in Julia's heart.

"Tracy, please don't say things like that. I understand it's a shock. But maybe Julia had a good reason for hiding this from us," their mother said.

"But that's the thing. She wasn't hiding it, really. She was just waiting for the worst possible time to tell us. I'm tired of her grandstanding. Every five minutes there's another fire to put out and it's all her doing."

Julia couldn't have moved if she'd wanted to. Her sister's words were consuming her whole, eating at her from the inside out. Her shoulders drooped; she closed her eyes, part of her wishing she could just psychically beam herself back to her New York apartment or to her house on the beach in Malibu. Anywhere else but here, where everyone was mad at her and her sister despised her very existence. She dared to open her eyes. Staring down, she was mocked by the field of billowy pink. *I'm here.*

Another knock came at the dressing room door. "Is everything okay in there?" Julia's father asked. "There's an awful lot of yelling. And did somebody say something about a baby?"

"I'll be right out, darling," Julia's mother answered, collecting her handbag. "I don't even know what to say," she said to Julia, her voice unsettled. "You know I don't like it when Tracy flies off the handle like this, but she's not wrong this time. You've created so much upheaval since your arrival."

Julia cast her eyes at her mother. The look on her face was difficult to pin a word to, but both *sad* and *disappointed* came to mind.

"I don't know what's going on with you, but I think you'd better get your act together, at least until this weekend is over. Otherwise, it's only going to get worse for all of us."

A puff of air left Julia's lips as she clutched that stupid bridesmaid's dress to her chest. She'd just told her mom that she was going to have a baby. It was a moment she'd thought about many times—one that was meant to be joyous and cheerful. Instead, she was standing in a fitting room, and it had come and gone in as unhappy a fashion as Julia could've imagined. It many ways, it mirrored her future…and her past, for that matter—the ways in which she couldn't stop messing up. "Aren't you going to say anything about the baby?"

Her mother's eyes were watery. "I'm excited for you sweetheart, really I am, but I'm in shock. And this really isn't a good time. I hope that we can talk about it later this weekend. After the wedding is over."

"Exactly why I wanted to keep the secret in the first place."

"How long have you known?"

"Three weeks. Or so."

"Three whole weeks? Oh, Jules. Three weeks?" She shook her head. "And you didn't tell me? Your sister would've been annoyed, but she would've been over it well before her wedding day arrived."

Julia sat down on the bench and buried her head in her hands. Her stomach burned as she realized that her mistake was much worse than she'd thought. "I'm so sorry. Really. I am. I didn't want it to be like this."

"I believe you. I do. Now we just need to wait for your sister to cool down. Speaking of which, let me see if I can find her and talk to her. And somebody's got to get your father up to speed."

"I'm coming with you." She had to fix this. She had to explain.

"It's probably best if you give your sister some space. I'm guessing you're the last person she wants to talk to."

Right now it felt as if there was an insurmountable divide between her Tracy. There was no telling how long it would take for her sister to calm down. When was the next ice age expected? That might be enough time.

"Let me talk to Daddy, then."

Her mother reached for the door. "I'll talk to him. He thinks you can do no wrong. He doesn't want to believe you might ever be untruthful with us. He'll probably be even more disappointed than I am that you kept this from us."

Disappointed. If ever there was a dagger to the heart of a child, that was it. She sat back and knocked her head against the wall as her mother closed the door. If she thought she'd felt alone in all of this when she arrived, she felt that tenfold now. She wrapped her arms around her waist, and the dress gaped in the back. All she wanted was someone on her side. All she wanted was someone who believed she'd had the best of intentions. All she wanted was someone who knew she was trying her best.

All she wanted was Logan.

Ten

After their trip to pick up the wedding bands, Logan and Carter pulled into the parking lot at the bridal boutique. Logan turned off the car and opened his door. Carter, however, seemed content to stay put.

"Everything okay?" Logan asked. "You've been quiet since we left the jeweler."

Carter nodded. "I'm good. Just thinking about everything. To be honest, I keep waiting for the other shoe to drop. When is my luck going to run out?"

Logan closed his door and turned the ignition on in order to roll down the windows. They might be there for a while. "I'm not sure I understand what you're saying. Are you getting cold feet? Because that's perfectly normal." *Hell, I'm the king of cold feet.*

Carter stared straight ahead as if he were pondering the very meaning of life. "When I'm with Tracy, I feel so lucky, especially thinking about the fact that we'd broken up for a whole year. What if she hadn't gotten a flat tire? What if I hadn't driven by her that day? We might never have gotten back together. My whole life turned around because of dumb luck."

"It's fate. Nothing dumb about it."

"I just think about what I would be doing right now if things hadn't turned out the way they did. I'd be living in my crappy condo, dragging myself to work every day, nothing to look forward to. I look at what that was like and I can't believe I lived through a single day of the year we were apart. It was pathetic."

Wow. Did that sound familiar—that was Logan's life. Sure, swap out the crappy condo for a sprawling home on a wooded lot in Connecticut with a pool and manicured grounds. And yes, he had an array of cars to choose from whenever it was time to head up to the network offices for a production meeting or to the airport to travel to a game, but his life was only a more glamorous version of bachelorhood than Carter's. At its essence, at its core, it was the same. And there was zero indication it was going to get any better. He dated some wonderful women, a pleasure to spend time with, but he never found himself wondering what was next, or even worrying whether they wanted to stick around. Whenever it came to a conclusion, it was almost always the same goodbye. *That was fun. Good luck. I hope you find the right woman someday.*

Logan reached over and grabbed Carter's shoulder. "You know, most guys don't appreciate what they have. Or they don't until it's too late. I'm glad you aren't one of those guys."

"So what about you? What about the stuff you were saying yesterday about not counting out the idea of you and Julia getting back together?"

Now it was Logan's turn to stare anywhere but at his best friend, choosing to fix his eyes on his own hands as he picked at his thumbnail. "I want us to try, but there are a lot of moving parts. I'm not sure it can happen until we resolve one or two things."

"No. Dude. Let me stop you right there. There is no resolving a few things. There are always going to be problems."

"Some problems are bigger than others." *Like having a thing for a woman who might be carrying another man's baby.*

"Listen to me. That day when Tracy got the flat tire? Do you think I was standing on the side of the road thinking about how much we used to fight? Or that she gets up at five and I can't sleep before midnight? Because I wasn't. All I was thinking about was how much I wanted to kiss her. All I was thinking about was how being with her felt right." Carter was clearly worked up about this—his cheeks were flushed and his blue eyes blazed.

"I see your point. You've given me a lot to think about."

"Look. You are my best friend in the whole world. You're the brother I never had. I want you to be happy. And you might have a lot of what most men want, but you don't have it all. I want that for you. If you love her, you have to lock things down with Jules. Otherwise, she gets on a plane on Monday morning and you two just go back to whatever in the heck you've been doing for the last dozen years. Tracy and I call it Olympic flirting. It makes the rest of us crazy to watch you two *not* figure it out."

Olympic flirting. He and Julia *were* really good at that.

Just then, Tracy burst out of the door to the boutique. The instant she saw Logan and Carter, she beelined for them, but she didn't go to her husband-to-be's side of the car. She went straight for Logan. "You. I don't know what your problem is, but I'm tired of this. First you dump her and then you get her pregnant?"

"Well, to be fair, it happened the other way around." Logan swallowed hard. What in the hell happened in the last forty-five minutes? And how bad was it going to be when he walked in there?

"Don't joke around about this. I'm in no mood. I'm telling you right now that you need to straighten things out with Julia." She leaned down and looked into the car at Carter. "Carter, honey. Please get me out of here. I just want to turn off my phone and eat ice cream and hang out with you. Everyone else is insane."

Carter practically leaped out of the car, rushing to Tracy's side, wrapping her up in his arms and kissing the top of her head. "Everything's going to be fine," he muttered to her. He then shot Logan the look he'd gotten far too many times since he'd arrived in North

Carolina. "Pregnant? And you're sitting in the car wondering what you should do?"

Logan was about to explain, or at least retort that it wasn't as simple as that, but he and Carter had already had that conversation. Enough talking in circles. "You two go. I'll tend to Julia." Logan climbed out of his car as Tracy and Carter got into hers.

He strode into the boutique. He had to shake his head when the door chime played "Here Comes the Bride." Mrs. Keys was standing at a counter, rummaging through her purse, while Mr. Keys looked on. Neither of them were pleased. In fact, Logan had never seen either of them look so unhappy. "Everything okay?" he asked, bracing for the answer.

"Sounds to me like you and Julia are the ones to answer that question." Mr. Keys's voice was stern and cold, a complete one-eighty from the way he'd greeted Logan on Wednesday.

"Logan? Is that you?" Julia stuck her head out from behind a door. She'd been crying. "Come here. We need to talk."

He looked at Julia's parents, desperate to explain. "Can we talk about this in one minute? Jules needs me right now."

"I'd say she needs you now more than anything. And we're on our way out." Mr. Keys ushered his wife out of the shop. She wouldn't even look at Logan.

He headed right over, stepping inside the dressing room. "What happened?"

She blew out an exasperated breath as she latched

the door. "My dress didn't fit and now everybody knows. Tracy is furious with me."

"Uh, yeah. I ran into her in the parking lot. I already got on the wrong end of your sister's fury."

"I didn't even have time to explain that I don't know for certain that you're the dad," she whispered. "Plus, I knew it was just going to make it worse. Tracy said the most awful things to me. She said she wished she hadn't asked me to be her maid of honor."

It felt as if ice ran through his veins. That was the worst possible thing Tracy could have said. "What do you want to do? Tell everybody the truth?"

"Surely it's occurred to you how messy the truth is."

"I've been thinking about little else since I first saw you on Wednesday." *And especially in the last ten minutes.*

Tears streamed down her face. "Do you want to know why I didn't do the paternity test? Because I knew that the minute I did, if you weren't the dad, you would never ever want anything to do with me again."

He pulled her into a hug, wishing he could squeeze the sadness out of her. "I would never feel that way." His mother had been absolutely right. This was the real thing holding Julia back. The breakup was one thing, but this was quite another. "We just have to get through the wedding. Tell me what you want to do and I'm on board with whatever it is. Okay?"

"Anything?"

"Anything."

She sucked in a breath and plopped down onto a bench, her dress poofing up around her. She looked as defeated as a person could be. It was no surprise. Her sister, the wedding, her parents…everyone and everything putting pressure on her in their own way. Never mind her worries about the baby. Logan had to give her whatever she wanted right now. It was only fair. He crouched down next to her, pushing aside the mounds of puffy pink dress. She sat straighter and peered into his eyes. Hers were so warm and inviting, sweet and vulnerable. They were like home.

"I just want everything to be okay. I want to feel safe. I want to feel normal. And happy," she said.

Logan reached out and wiped the tears away from her cheek. They were welling in his eyes, too. "I hate seeing you cry, Jules. It kills me."

"I'm sorry."

"I don't want you to be sorry. Please. Stop being sorry."

Again, she sought his eyes. In some ways it felt as if they were having a conversation that was separate from the one that came from their lips. Every part of him wanted to wrap his arms around her and take her away. He took her hand, grasping her delicate fingers. The irony that they were in a bridal boutique while he had his grandmother's ring in his pocket was not lost on him. He would've popped it out and brought her to tears for an entirely different reason if he didn't know that it would take baby steps with Julia. He had to open his heart to her. If he was having a hard time trusting her, she felt the same way.

"Let me keep you safe," he said. "Let me make things normal. We'll get through the wedding, and then we'll talk about everything when the pressure is off. I think we need to take some of the drama out of your life."

"It's not polite to have the bride kidnapped." A slight smile crossed her face. She pulled up the neckline of her dress, trying to hitch it up. "So you're going to have to tell me what you mean."

"Everyone already thinks we're together. And now your parents and Tracy know about the baby. And between the hotel room this morning and everything that happened in the car this afternoon, you and I both know that staying away from each other never works. Neither one of us is very good at it."

"Yeah. I noticed."

"So let's just try to be together. For two days. Let's be Julia and Logan. Together. A couple. No putting on a show."

"What will we do if people ask us about it? Because you know they're going to. They're going to ask about the baby and whether we're getting married. And I don't think I can pretend about that. I need it to be real."

"We'll just say that we're together and we're focused on Tracy and Carter right now. That's the truth, and if that's not good enough for them, then too bad. We'll just have to walk away or get really good at changing the subject."

"What do we tell everyone later? After the wedding?"

He took her other hand and gripped them together tightly. They were both putting a lot on the line here, willingly creating a tangle that could become an unholy mess to clean up. It didn't matter. Their past was littered with mistakes that couldn't be undone and their future was uncertain at best, but it was theirs. And it was up to the two of them to figure it out. "All we can do is our best right now. If anyone wants to fault us for that after the fact, then that's their problem. And if someone needs to take the heat, I will."

"You don't have to do that. I can take it. I'm used to it."

"You know what? I don't want you to be used to it. Let me shield you from this."

Julia swallowed. "Do you have any idea how many times I've had a guy say he'd stick up for me like that?"

He shrugged. "No idea. You know it's not my favorite subject."

"Zero. Zero times. You're the only one."

"Really?"

"Really. Believe me, I wouldn't lie about that." She stood and hiked up her dress again. "Okay. Let me get out of this silly get-up so we can get it to the seamstress and she can hopefully finish the alterations before tomorrow. I need to get out of this place."

He straightened, now keenly aware of the privacy they had, in a way that hadn't made an impression before. He really wanted to kiss her again. "I don't get to stay?"

She shook her head. "We're in a bridal boutique in the South. Let's not invite more scandal into our lives by being the unmarried pregnant couple making out in the fitting room."

His hand nearly twitched. The ring in his pocket might help to shut everyone up. But he couldn't go there until he knew for certain that she would say yes, and that they were ready. They needed their trial period. They needed to lean on each other again. "Okay, then. Out I go."

Logan quietly exited the dressing room and closed the door behind him. A few steps into the main room of the boutique and the eyes of the women working at the shop were all on him. He was used to women staring at him every now and then, but this was different. There was a whole lot of judgment being aimed at him right now and he didn't like it one bit. Julia thankfully emerged from behind the white door, the pink dress in her hands. One of the women working in the shop rushed over to take it from her.

A fraction of a smile crossed Julia's face as she walked up to him. Relief settled in. As much as she needed reassurance that everything would be okay, he needed it, too. He wasn't going to ask for it, but hopefully that grin from her meant that he could start trusting his instincts again. It was time.

"So? What should we do?" he asked. "We have hours until we need to be at the rehearsal."

"You know what would be awesome?"

Logan hoped she would suggest they go back to the hotel and have sex all afternoon.

"Let's go to the beach."

Eleven

Julia rolled down the car window and leaned against the door frame, letting the wind sweep her hair from her face and the sun warm her skin. Closing her eyes, she breathed in the familiar salty breeze.

"Any particular place you want to stop?" Logan asked.

"Anywhere quiet. I do not want to see people. And if you see a single member of my family, turn around and go in the opposite direction. I don't care how fast you drive."

He laughed, further improving her mood. If ever there was a sound worth listening to, it was Logan's laugh—not as deep as his speaking voice, but close, and it was always unguarded. "If we want privacy, then I think we both know where we need to go."

Privacy. "Yes. Go there."

A short fifteen minutes later, Logan pulled the car over to the side of the road in the perfect spot, right where a long string of rental houses stood between two of the bigger beach hotels. The undertow was particularly strong in this stretch and the sand extra pebbly, making it far less popular with swimmers. With school back in session, it wouldn't be too busy.

Julia kicked off her flats and collected them in her hands while Logan sat on the edge of the public access walkway, taking off his black leather shoes and removing his socks. He rolled up the legs of his jeans. Julia just watched, admiring him. A stunning ocean vista might have been waiting on the other side of the dunes, but the line of Logan's athletic shoulders as he hunched over was more enticing. He stood and gathered his things in one hand, while doing something that she had once taken for granted. He reached for her. Surely he'd done it thousands of times over the years, but it nearly knocked the breath out of her now. So much was expressed in that single gesture—everything she'd wished for, the thing that had left an unimaginable void when it was taken away. She'd felt heartbroken every time she and Logan had ever parted, even when she'd done the walking away.

"Hey, Logan," she said as they advanced over rickety gray wooden slats glazed with sand. Tall beach grass rustled and whipped at their legs. "Can we make a deal?"

"Tentatively, yes."

She stepped ahead of him and came to a stop, tak-

ing his other hand and peering up at him. His aviator
sunglasses glinted as a curious smile spread slowly
across his lips. Between the glare and his grin, it was
a wonder she wasn't blind. "No more questions today,
okay? Even when it's just the two of us. Let's practice
being happy. I think I've forgotten how to do that."

He wrapped an arm around her shoulders, pulling
her close and pressing a kiss to the top of her head. At
moments like this, his tenderness was unmatched, a
gift. "I think we both could use the practice."

Julia sighed, her legs feeling a bit like they were
made of rubber. Being in his arms gave her exactly
what she'd been craving—a refuge. "Good."

A few dozen steps and they crested the dunes and
descended the stairs to the beach. Aside from an older
couple sleeping on lounge chairs beneath an umbrella
and a man casting a line into the water, the shore was
nearly deserted, stretching north for what looked like
a mile without another person. Julia let Logan lead
the way down to the water. Midafternoon, the tide
was low, revealing millions of tiny shells and scat-
tered strands of seaweed.

Julia ventured in to her ankles, but Logan went
midcalf, tugging on her hand. "Come on," he insisted.
"It's so warm today."

"I don't want to get my dress wet."

He shook his head. "Don't be lame. Just come
here."

There was something so sexy about being beck-
oned by Logan, somewhere between the tempting
trouble of a dare and the thrill of an irresistible man

wanting you close. She waded deeper. She had to. There was no denying Logan. Not when he was like this. She stood right next to him, the waves indeed threatening to soak the hem of her dress. They both looked off at the horizon, holding hands, leaning into each other as the Atlantic lapped at their legs. His thumb rubbed the back of her hand in a steady rhythm. The sun warmed her shoulders. Between Logan and the rock of the tide, the stress and worry were slipping away.

"Are you ready to give your toast tomorrow?" she asked.

"Yep. I have it all typed on my phone and everything."

"How very efficient of you."

"The best man should be prepared."

"I, of course, went old school and wrote mine on paper. I'm a little worried it's corny, though. Either that or I'm thinking too hard about it."

"Do you have it with you?" He tugged on her hand.

"I do. It's in my purse. Want to trade?"

"We should probably at least practice."

"On dry land?"

"Yes."

They took their time, Julia kicking at the water as they made their way back up onto shore. They found a dry patch of sand and sat. The wind blew Julia's hair in a million directions as she dug around in her purse for the paper. Amid lip balm, gum and a pack of tissues, she finally found the carefully folded sheet torn from a legal pad. She handed it to Logan as he surrendered his phone to her.

It came as no surprise that Logan's was pure poetry from the first word, but the real curiosity was his subject matter. A few sentences in, she had to say something. "Logan. This is practically the same thing I wrote. Well, I mean, yours is written far better than mine, but that's no shock. You know, you really should write a memoir. I wasn't trying to fix your problems when I suggested it."

"I wouldn't know where to start with that, and I'm not sure anyone would want to read it in the first place."

"But you're an amazing writer. You'd figure it out. I know you'd do a fantastic job."

He returned his sights to the page, which ruffled in the breeze. Forearms resting on his knees, he shook his head and smiled. "Shhh. I'm reading."

Like she was supposed to do the same when he was being so adorable. Still, she returned to what he'd written, just to hear his voice in her head. It only took a few more lines before goose bumps were racing up her bare arms, even in the glow of the fading sun. "Fate returning two souls to each other? Isn't that the exact same thing I said?"

"You said fate *bringing* two souls together."

"Of course. I don't have your flair, Mr. Memoir-Writer. I'm calling you that from now on, just so you know." She went on reading, soon stumbling over another parallel. "We both told the same story, about that night at the beach house when Tracy cut her foot on that rusty old can in the sand. About Carter carrying her inside and how sweet they were to each other."

"Is it really that surprising? It's a great story."

She shrugged. "It is a great story, but it also happened an eon ago. It's still a weird coincidence."

"When you and I are on the same page, we're really on the same page."

Julia's skin tingled with recognition. "It's true. There's not much stopping us when we're in sync." She handed him his phone and tucked her speech back into her purse. "Yours is so good. It's almost too good. I feel like I should change mine. Otherwise people are just going to get bored or say that we copied each other."

"Yours is perfect. Keep it just the way it is. I'll tweak mine. I'm sure I can come up with something else to say."

"See? You can't *not* write." Julia leaned back on her hands, digging her toes into the sand. "You know, I think about that night with Tracy and Carter and I'm still sort of in awe of it. It's still so vivid. It was like watching a movie. We saw them fall in love with each other. It was so romantic."

He reached back for her hand. "Maybe we're watching the same thing."

Warmth rushed to her cheeks. "It's not the same. We're participating. And we're a lot older now. We already fell in love for the first time."

"First off, I think it's better that we're older. It means more. And people can fall in love more than once. My grandmother used to say that the secret to a long marriage was falling in love over and over again. She'd been married to my grandfather for sixty-seven years when he passed away."

Leave it to Logan to break out an especially poignant story, made even better with his impossibly romantic turn of phrase. As competitive as they could be with each other, she'd gladly be outmatched by him when it came to romance. "Yeah? What makes you think things will suddenly work now that it's all so much more complicated?"

He shook his head and raised a finger to her lips. "We aren't asking questions today. No worrying about tomorrow. We only do what makes us happy. We do what feels right." He moved his hand to the side of her face and raked his fingers through her hair. "Like this."

Her heart wouldn't stop fluttering at the anticipation as he rubbed her jaw with his thumb and caressed her neck with his fingers. When his lips finally met hers, the kiss was soft and tender, but passionate. Focused. She sensed a different sweet sentiment with every move of his mouth, which still amazed her, even after all this time. She arched her back, craned her neck, desperate to keep doing the one thing that they knew they couldn't get wrong, no matter how hard they tried. His lips became more insistent, the heat building, his tongue gentle but unsubtle in where this was going. He wasn't kidding about doing what felt right—this was every kind of correct she could imagine. She shut out the bad thoughts that wanted to creep in and went with the moment. Old wounds would take a long time to heal. She couldn't expect it to happen overnight. And the kiss was definitely helping.

Logan really wished they had a blanket, so they could lie back on the sand, roll around a little. But they didn't, which meant he could take this kiss only so far. Not to mention that they were in public, however quiet the beach was that afternoon.

Julia's lips were as sweet now as they'd been every other time he'd kissed her over the last few days, but there was something else behind the kiss now...a promise that they were going to try to find a way. If Julia would just give a little bit, try to understand his hesitation and at least acknowledge that it was okay for him to feel the way he did, he could do the same. Give an inch here, an inch there, until finally they could meet in the middle.

Her hand clutched his biceps, her hair whipped at his face, as they both became more emphatic with the kiss. It was as if they were in their own little world and they were doing nothing but one-upping each other, a familiar part of their dynamic. *I want you. I want you more. I want you the most.* Logan's brain wouldn't stop thinking about what might lie ahead...a continuation of the heavenly fun they'd had that morning. They did, after all, have a hotel room to return to. They did, after all, have several hours until the rehearsal.

Julia's phone started beeping in her purse. She

wrenched herself from the kiss and turned away from him, grabbing at her bag and digging in it.

"No, Jules. Let it go." *This is too good.* His eyes were half-open, his breathing labored. Every part of him was poised and ready to have her, make love to her.

"It's not a call. It's the alarm on my phone. We should head back to the hotel to get ready for the rehearsal."

The hotel. Bed. Privacy. "Yes. We should go." Logan grabbed his shoes and stood up, even when it was difficult to fully straighten. Everything below his waist was ready to have her, and it felt as if the blood had left his limbs. Julia scampered up the dunes to the stairs and Logan had no choice but to follow, every step painful, especially as he watched the sway of her hips in that summery dress and the way the wind carried it up to the middle of her thighs.

Logan grabbed a pair of flip-flops he'd left in the back seat and put them on, wanting to hurry as much as Julia did. He started the car and cranked the air-conditioning, needing to cool off. Julia had him way too warmed up. That morning had been wonderful, but it wasn't nearly enough, and everything had been a mystery then. There was far less gray area between them now.

They arrived at the hotel in record time, but Julia didn't seem to notice the liberties he'd taken with the speed limit. She was preoccupied with texting and checking things on her phone. The guy at the valet stand greeted them and took care of the car quickly, and they lucked out when they didn't have to wait for the elevator inside. Down the hall to their room, each step only made Logan's pulse race faster. He would have her. Right now.

He took her into his arms the instant they were inside their room, his hand quickly finding the zipper on the back of her dress and drawing it down. She kissed him back, moaning softly. He loved the sound, until he realized it was a complaint.

"Everything okay?"

"Why did you have to kiss me at the beach that way?" Her gorgeous chest was heaving.

"We were going with it, remember? And being around you is making me crazy, Jules. I want you. Now."

"I know. I want you, too." She kissed him, her tongue winding with his. "But we can't. There's no time. If we're late for the rehearsal, Tracy will literally kill me."

Julia's moans might have conveyed annoyance, but he was about to register a grievance of his own. "Just a quickie. Or a shower. We'll call it multitasking."

She shook her head and kissed his cheek. "You're cute, but I have to do my hair and makeup from scratch and I haven't shaved my legs."

"See? I'll help."

"Do you really want to rush through this? If we're going to make love do you really want to hurry it? After the day we've had and everything we said to each other?" She pressed her hand flat against his chest. "I want us to be able to take our time with each other." She bit on her lower lip. "I want to be able to be thorough. If you know what I mean."

A low rumble came from the center of his chest. Oh, he knew exactly what she meant. And thinking about it all night was going to make him insane. Still, she was probably right. If they were going to get back to where they used to be, it needed to be more than a quickie. They needed hours to reconnect on every level. "Okay. You shower first. Just be sure to use all of the hot water. Every drop. I want mine ice cold."

"I'm sorry. Really. I am." She popped up onto her tiptoes and kissed his cheek. She flashed a smile and hurried off to the bathroom, shutting the door behind her.

Logan flopped down on the bed, frustration about to eat him alive. *This is going to be a really, really long night.*

Twelve

Logan now knew what it was like to be on the outs with the Keys family. And he didn't like it one bit.

"I have to talk to your dad," he mumbled into Julia's ear as they both stood in the church, waiting for the rehearsal to start.

"Not now," she whispered.

"At dinner."

She shot him a look. "Can we talk about this later?"

He was about to retort that they'd agreed there would be no questions, but the minister had begun delivering orders. Stand here. Stand there. Walk like this. Wait for this. Get out the rings. Wait again. This was going to take forever. All while enduring the cold shoulder from Julia's parents.

Carter and Tracy were wound as tight as he'd seen either of them, but it was seeing Mr. and Mrs. Keys like this that really ate at him. If he and Julia were going to find a future, he couldn't be at odds with them. Surprisingly, the person who seemed somewhat relaxed, or at least comparatively so, was Julia. Whether she'd wanted to admit it or not, keeping the secret of the baby had been a big burden to bear.

By far, the high spot of the rehearsal was standing at the altar with the other groomsmen, watching Julia walk up the aisle. Step by measured step, she was both graceful and statuesque, wearing a gauzy navy blue dress that fluttered at her feet and showed off her gorgeous shoulders. Their gazes connected, and he couldn't have contained his grin if he'd wanted to. Similarly, a smile broke across her face; petal pink washed over her cheeks. She shied away, casting her sights to the red carpet runner. His mind raced with excuses they could use to skip the rehearsal dinner—a horrible headache, a painful splinter. The truth was that he and Julia had shared a roller coaster of a day—from the high points of making love and spending time on the beach, to the low of that moment in the fitting room. They were finally back on track. She knew how he felt about the things that had bothered him for years, and he had begun the process of accepting that he might not be the baby's father. He'd been working hard to see past that possibility. And because of the things they'd patched up today, he craved more togetherness. He longed for them to be alone.

Once the ceremony run-through was done, and

the bride and groom had shared their practice kiss, it was time for Logan and Julia to walk down the aisle arm in arm.

"You are so beautiful in that dress," he muttered out of the side of his mouth, pulling her close. "I know I told you at the hotel, but really. It's mind-boggling."

"You told me in the car, too. And don't act like I can even come close to matching the way you look in that suit." She glanced up at him, putting every nerve ending in his body on high alert. "The tie really brings out your eyes. Much better than the ones they put you in on TV."

Damn, it felt good to be admired by her. It was intoxicating enough to be in her presence, but when she was solely focused on him? Forget it. The rest of the world hardly existed. Step by step down that aisle, all eyes on them, he couldn't help but wonder what it would be like to go through this ritual with her. He had some fences to mend with the Keyses, but that would pass. With the ring in his pocket, he was still waiting to find the right moment to ask, the perfect point in time. There'd been twelve years of build-up to a proper proposal. It had to be right, and it had to be romantic.

Would Julia be as much of a wreck for her own wedding as she was for her sister's? He could just see it now—guest list a mile long, a wedding planner buzzing about and bossing everyone around, a big fancy church and an even fancier reception. Between her Hollywood friends and his legion of former teammates, it did seem to call for a grand affair. One rule would have to be strictly adhered to, by both of them—no exes. No exceptions.

Tracy insisted Julia ride with her out to the beach house for dinner, which left Carter and Logan some guy time in Logan's car.

"I can't believe you didn't tell me about the baby," Carter said. "That's huge."

He and Julia didn't enjoy the business of keeping secrets, but they had agreed to keep the question of paternity under wraps for now. They had enough obstacles to overcome, and they didn't need the world weighing in on their future. "I know. I'm sorry. I promised her I wouldn't say anything and I had to keep my word."

"Are you nervous? First-time dad and you have to figure out a way to make things work with the one woman who makes you crazy? That's a big challenge."

Logan felt the corners of his mouth turn down. It was so much more than that, and Carter had no idea. "When you put it like that, yes. I'm nervous."

"I didn't mean to sound all gloom-and-doom. I'm just in awe of you for trying. I think it's awesome. You're going to make an amazing dad."

Logan took the left onto Lumina Avenue toward the Keyses' beach house. Carter's words were still ringing in his ears. Was he really going to make a good dad? He wanted to think so. He wanted to believe he was up to the challenge, even if it meant raising a child who wasn't biologically his. "If I can be half as good of a dad as my father was, I'll be doing pretty well."

"I'm bummed I never had a chance to meet your dad. He sounds like he was such an incredible man."

"He was. I never would've gotten as far in baseball as I did without the things he did for me. I just wish I could've done it all. I still feel like I let him down. Or at least his memory." Logan always missed his dad, but it was especially palpable today. The conversation he'd had with his mom that morning would've been different with his father. Backward or macho or whatever anyone wanted to call it, his dad would've understood Logan's perspective fully. He wanted the baby to be his.

"I don't see any way your dad would've been anything less than totally proud of you."

"I guess. But if we'd won the World Series, I wouldn't have any doubts."

Logan slowed down as they approached the Keyses' beach house, which was all lit up, glowing against the darkening night sky. The parking area under the house was full, so Logan took a spot on the road. He turned off the ignition. "Ready?"

"I want to say one more thing. I know it's only been a year, but you need to find a way to let this go. Stop being so hard on yourself."

It wasn't that Logan needed the affirmation, but he'd take it. "Do I need to start paying you by the hour? Or are you hoping for a future in career counseling for athletes?"

Carter laughed. "I get that you're competitive and

that you want it all. But not every ballplayer wins a World Series. Not every dad has a chance to see his child fulfill their dreams. It's sad, but it's life."

I know. Do I ever know.

Tracy pulled up behind them. Logan and Carter quickly hopped outside. Carter walked double-time to Tracy's side of the car, opening her door for her. By the time Logan got to Julia, he was too late to do the same, but he was at least able to close it for her. Tracy and Carter made their way to the house; Logan and Julia lagged behind.

"When do we get to get out of here?" he muttered.

"We haven't even eaten yet. My sister will freak out if we leave early."

"I know, but all I want is to be alone with you."

She stopped just shy of the door. A sly smile crossed her lips. "You're cute when you're desperate for sex."

"I'm not desperate. Just ready." It was about more than the physical urge, though. He needed that connection with her, especially after everything today.

He wrapped his arm around her waist and pulled her forward. Julia kissed him this time and it was so natural, as if they were falling together in perfect sync. It was as if he'd stepped into a dream. She pressed into him, arching her back, hinting at everything he wanted with a welcome side of enthusiasm.

They went inside where everyone was gathering for dinner—aunts, uncles and distant cousins had arrived at the house during the rehearsal, with their Aunt Judy, who lived up the coast in Elizabeth City, in charge. Lined up neatly on the kitchen island were chafing dishes of North Carolina chopped pork barbecue, coleslaw, hush puppies, collard greens and baked beans. Logan's stomach growled, but something else inside him begged for attention as he again exchanged looks with Julia's dad. He had to speak to him.

After dinner and many long toasts, Logan saw Julia's dad step outside onto the deck. Julia was immersed in conversation with her aunt, so he took his chance. He didn't want an argument. He wanted to fix this.

"Mr. Keys," Logan said, closing the sliding glass door behind him. The night air was humid and blustery. "Do you have a minute?"

Mr. Keys was standing at the railing, looking out at the surf. "Always. I always have a minute for you."

Logan finally felt as though he could breathe. "About today. I know this all came as a shock, but I don't want everyone to be too hard on Julia. She really was doing what she felt was right. You know her. She's always worried far more about everyone else than she is about herself."

Mr. Keys let out a quiet laugh. "I do know that about my daughter. That's for sure. She's been like that since she was little. The number of stray animals she brought home over the years would make your head spin. And don't even get me started on the charity lemonade stands."

Now it was Logan's turn to laugh. He loved the image of a young Julia, out there, trying to save the world one project at a time.

"So is this what you were hinting at yesterday?" Mr. Keys asked. "That business of not counting you two out?"

Logan nodded. "You could say that. I know this is unconventional, but things with Julia and I have been rocky over the years. We're doing our best to put it together."

"Unconventional? I'd call it putting the cart before the horse." Mr. Keys's words nearly made Logan's heart seize up. He turned, leaning back against the railing and folding his arms across his chest. He nodded in the direction of the party inside. Julia and Tracy were talking, right on the other side of the sliding glass doors. "You'll understand it much better when you're a dad, but those two girls are my greatest gift. I would do anything to protect them. Keep them safe."

"I understand. I really do."

"But you know, what you and Julia do is none of my darn business. I just want my daughters to be happy." There was an unmistakable wobble to Mr. Keys's voice, underscoring the reasons he'd been testy with Logan.

"I admire you for doing anything to protect your girls."

"I have to admit, I'm more than a little excited by the prospect of being a grandfather." He elbowed Logan in the stomach. "And what if it's a boy? I could have a major leaguer for a grandson."

Logan caught the look in Mr. Keys's eye, a glint of pride. Something about that moment made the baby much more real, far less of an abstract. Would the baby be a boy? A girl? Regardless, he saw ten small fingers and ten small toes, chubby legs and cheeks, a sweet baby face. In his mind, his head, and his heart, the baby looked like both Julia and him. He couldn't see the baby any other way. It might not be the right vision to cling to, but it was an idea firmly planted, and he'd just have to deal with the reality when the time came.

"I want you to know that I won't let Julia down. And I won't shirk my responsibilities. You'll have to trust that we're doing our best to work things out." He watched Julia through the glass—the way she focused intently when someone spoke to her, the way she tossed her head back when she laughed, and the way her smile reflected the light inside her. She was so beautiful, inside and out. Mr. Keys had called her a gift. Logan understood now how true that was. *I love her.* He wasn't sure what he'd done to be lucky enough to have a second chance with her. Or in reality, more like his tenth chance. He only knew that he wouldn't let Julia wonder whether he was there for her. She said she needed to feel safe and like everything was okay. He could do that.

After two plates of food, three lemonades and countless uncomfortable questions about the future, Julia allowed herself to relish the part she'd played in making the rehearsal dinner a success. Tracy had completed the process of softening to her sister, although it had taken some intense conversation during the car ride to the beach, topped off with Tracy downing several glasses of wine. She actually seemed happy with the way things had gone. The food had been wonderful; the cake had arrived on time and exactly as Tracy had wanted it. Everyone raved about the house renovations. Tracy even remarked that the decorations were "perfect." Aside from an uncle from Indiana liberating himself from his pants before heading out for a late-night swim, the evening had been largely free of controversy. Now the final guests were filtering out of the beach house.

Julia was helping clean up the kitchen when Logan came up behind her, wrapping his arms around her waist and kissing her neck. "Mmm. You smell so good." His words and a single kiss sent electricity racing along her spine. And it felt so good to have his broad frame and warm body pressed against hers.

"Thank you. Shouldn't be too long and we can get out of here. Just a few more dishes."

"Can't someone else deal with this? You've worked your butt off today." With that, he gave her bottom a gentle squeeze. "Save some for me, please."

Julia turned around and playfully swatted him on his arm. "You're bad."

"I said please." His eyes scanned her face, amping up the anticipation. Sure, she and Logan had been to bed before. Just that morning, in fact. But not like this. Not when so much was on the line and she was so very well aware of how easily it could fall apart. She decided it was best to celebrate the fragile nature of what was between them. It was new life, just like the baby, and that was to be nurtured and cared for.

"Aunt Judy, do you mind finishing up?" Julia asked.

Her aunt looked up from the living room where she was fluffing couch cushions and picking up plastic cups. "Of course, darling. I'll take care of it. See you in the morning at the church."

"Have I told you how much I adore you, Aunt Judy?" Logan asked.

"You didn't need to. It's all over your face." She smiled wide. "Now shoo, you two."

Julia grabbed her purse and cardigan, took Logan's hand, and out they went into the night. The roar of the ocean was off in the distance, warm breeze sweeping against her skin as Logan took her hand and led her to the car. They climbed inside and Logan went for a kiss instead of turning the key in the ignition.

Julia reared back her head. "If we start here, we'll never be able to leave. And I really don't want Aunt Judy walking by while we're steaming up the windows."

"So true." Logan started the car, and after quickly looking both ways, made a U-turn in the middle of the street and raced off to the hotel. This late at night, they thankfully hit more than their fair share of green lights. Julia hoped it was symbolic of the future—no more stopping. Just moving forward.

By the time they turned the car over to the valet, speed-walked through the lobby, rode the elevator and raced down the hall to their room, they were both laughing. It was a fun and nervous laughter, filled with hope and happiness. Julia couldn't think of a time when things had felt more perfect.

"Before we go in, phones off," he said.

"Yes. You're so smart." She dug hers from her purse and shut the power off. "Good to go."

Logan opened the door and had his hands all over her the instant it closed behind them. "This dress has got to go."

"I thought you liked it."

"I do. I love it. I love it so much I want to see what it looks like on the floor. I think it will go with the carpet quite nicely."

"Just like your suit."

"I feel like we should hang up the suit."

"And not my dress? Talk about a double standard."

He wrapped his hand around her neck and rubbed her jaw with his thumb. "Kiss me and tell me we can worry about laundry later."

"Gladly," she purred, tugging on his necktie as his mouth crashed into hers. He smelled so good—the fragrance she could only describe as Logan, like a good glass of bourbon, warmed in the summer sun.

She took off his tie and he wrestled his way out of his jacket. Her fingers flew over the buttons of his shirt and as soon as that was gone, he turned her around, unzipping the back of her dress. He teased it from her shoulders, pushing it to the floor before pressing his body against hers. She felt the cool metal of his belt buckle in the curve of her back, and lower…a firm declaration of how turned on he was. He took her hair in his hands and swept it back from her neck, kissing her softly with a gentle brush of his tongue. She loved having him stand behind her. There was something so sexy about it, as if he expected no reciprocity, but of course she would be giving.

She reached back, finding his erection, which strained against the front of his pants. She pressed against it with her hand, eliciting a low groan from him. He backed up slightly and unhooked her strapless bra, a double dose of relief—the boning had been digging into her armpits for hours. She hummed with happiness over the reprieve from the torturous garment. Logan turned her in his arms, admiring her breasts with both hands, both eyes and a whole lot of commentary.

"I've always loved your breasts, but I just love how full they are right now."

Heat rushed to her cheeks. "Thanks."

"I meant it. They're stunning. Truly stunning."

"I'm glad you're enjoying them."

He cupped them with his palms, rubbed her nipples with his thumbs, drawing them into tight peaks. A week or so ago, that would've been torture, but the initial tenderness had subsided and between his touch and the pregnancy hormones, she was writhing with anticipation of more. As if he'd heard the wish she'd made in her head, he lowered his head and drew a nipple into his warm mouth, sucking softly and flicking at it with his tongue. She cradled his head in her hands, caressing his temples, leaning down to kiss the top of his head. He switched to the other breast and did the same, ramping up the intensity with licks and hot breath, causing her skin to bead so tightly she already felt as if she might unravel the instant he touched her most intimate parts.

He lowered himself to his knees, clutching her rib cage, then dragging his hands down her sides to her hips. He kissed her lower belly, gazing up at her. The only light in the room came from the nearly full moon, which was low in the sky tonight and cast soft beams through the window sheers. He was unbearably handsome in any light, but she couldn't have imagined him looking any more so than he did at that moment—his eyes and face full of adoration.

"I meant what I said earlier about your current state being a turn-on. Your body is so ripe right now. Every inch of you has a little more to squeeze and I love it. I absolutely love it." He grasped her hips, curving his fingers into the fleshy part of her buttocks, then tucked his fingers into the waist of her black satin panties and dragged them down to her ankles. She stepped out of them, reaching out to the arm of the chair behind her to steady herself. Logan seized the opportunity and backed her up a step, urging her to sit, but making it clear with his hands that he wanted her perched on the edge of the seat. Still on his knees, he coaxed one of her legs outward and hitched the other leg over his shoulder, opening her up to him. "Sit back for me," he said.

She watched his every move as his hand found her center and teased apart the folds. She gasped when he slipped two fingers inside her and rocked his thumb against her apex, slowly but deliberately. Her eyes opened and closed in an unpredictable pattern as her mind warred between wanting to luxuriate in the pleasure and wanting to watch what this incredible man was able to do to her. His fingers continued to glide inside her, and he curled them into the spot that made her arch her back and moan. Every inch of her marveled at how good it all felt, but there was a whole lot of anticipation of the main event going on in her head. "That feels so good," she muttered, feeling as if she might break at any moment. "But I want you inside me, Logan."

He kissed her lower belly. "I love hearing you say that. But we have all night, and I plan to enjoy every inch of you." He then moved his thumb aside from the tender bundle of nerves he'd been working and lowered his mouth to that spot, enveloping her with warmth as he wound his tongue in lazy circles.

Her thoughts were hazy, pleasure coiling tightly in her belly, and all she could do was unwind and let Logan have his way. Her breaths were ragged. Her chest heaved. Her body temperature was climbing steadily, warming her skin. With every pass of his tongue, the release crept closer, until finally she could take the pressure no longer and gave in to the orgasm. She called out his name and grasped his head, as every wave of joy and warmth unraveled her a little more. The minute she got her wits back, she sat up and brought Logan's face to hers, kissing him deeply as the remnants of the release still teased her body. In some ways, he hadn't satisfied her need for him so much as he'd heightened it.

He rose to his feet and stood before her, a tower of defined muscle. She tugged him closer and wrapped her hand around his steely length, rolling her thumb over the tip and watching his reaction. He closed his eyes and his head dropped back as her fingers rode up and down, gripping him until he became impossibly hard.

"Make love to me, Logan," she whispered.

He reached down and took her hand, bringing her to standing. They wrapped their arms around each other, kissing deeply, lips warm and wet. They turned in circles on their way to the bed, an incoherent couple's dance that eventually brought them to their landing spot. They collapsed on the bed in a heap and Logan rolled her to her back. He positioned himself between her legs and pushed himself up with one arm. Julia gasped when he finally came inside, at first only a little, before he flexed his torso and thrust with one strong and fluid movement.

He kissed her passionately, his tongue exploring her mouth and lips, as she wrapped her legs around him and they rocked in a rhythm that was all their own. Julia's mind became a swirl of serene thoughts. Many things in her world had felt wrong lately, but this undoubtedly felt right. It was the one conclusion she could make with zero deliberation. Logan rode in and out of her, lowering his head to her breast and flicking at her nipples with his tongue.

She was already poised for another release, but she focused on relaxing, even when her body was tensing in waves. His breaths were becoming short and labored, and she could tell from the tension in his back that he was close to his own climax. He kissed her again, this time with reckless urgency, his open mouth skating over hers, her cheeks and her neck. His thrusts came faster and more forceful until finally his body froze and a deep groan left his throat. He shuddered in her arms, and that was all it took for her to come undone once more, her body clutching his as he took a few final thrusts.

In utter exhaustion, he collapsed next to her on the bed, not hesitating to pull her against him and kiss her softly. "That was so incredible. Totally worth the wait."

She laughed quietly and shook her head, resting her head on his magnificent chest. "You mean the wait since this morning?"

"This morning was wonderful, don't get me wrong. But this had a lot of build-up. Makes it better." He raked his fingers through her hair. "I want you to know one thing, Jules. I have always loved you. No matter what happens, I always will."

The confession took her by surprise, but not of a happy nature. It left her with that familiar sinking feeling, mostly because of what he hadn't said recently. Ever since they'd been doing well as a pair, he'd dropped all of his talk of marriage. What did that mean? Was he just trying to get through the weekend? He'd been so insistent about it before, bringing it up whenever he had the chance. Now the subject of marriage, and the future, and the baby were all absent. "You never stopped?"

Logan groaned. "Jules. No questions, remember?"

But she did have a question. More than one, actually. Starting with this—why did "I will always love you" have to sound so much like "goodbye"?

Thirteen

Waking up next to Julia was more spectacular than Logan had remembered. Perhaps because it meant more now. They had managed to reclaim what they had three months ago, only this time he would not mess up.

She stirred in his arms and kissed his chest, bringing his entire body to life. "Good morning," she murmured sweetly.

"It is a very good morning." *Every morning will be good with you.*

"The big day is here."

"It is." The big day was indeed upon them, and not just for Tracy and Carter, although Julia had no idea. Logan had monumental plans for after the wedding—he was finally going to propose. He'd decided last night after Jules fell asleep, spending hours—literally—thinking out every scenario. The way he might feel if the baby wasn't his. The way he would feel if the baby was. What it would feel like to build a family with Julia, the woman he'd never stop loving. He wouldn't take this lightly, as she'd suggested he might. He was ready. They were ready. He would convince her of it. And he was an idiot if he waited even another day. He wasn't about to risk something going wrong. He had to tie up these particular loose strings, ASAP.

"Yep. Won't be long now and it'll all be over. I'll be flying back to LA to finish the movie. You'll be flying home to Connecticut."

He could tease her about this later, right after he'd popped the question. "Back to reality."

She abruptly sat up in bed, turning her back to him. "Have you figured out what you're changing in your toast?"

"Not yet, but I will." With everything else going on, he hadn't had a spare second to think about it. Hopefully something would happen during the ceremony to spark an idea.

She grabbed his T-shirt from the floor and put it on, then made a beeline for the bathroom.

"You aren't leaving me, are you?"

"Gotta hop in the shower. It's my last chance to have an entire day where I don't make my sister mad. I don't want us to be late."

She closed the bathroom door and Logan got up, pulling on a pair of basketball shorts. He began to collect the belongings he would need for the day. He reached inside the pants pocket where the ring was safely tucked away, and gave it a squeeze for good luck. Wouldn't be long until it was on Julia's finger.

Julia had left a tote bag sitting on the floor, which had fallen over, causing several things to slip out, including a book about pregnancy. Curious, he flipped through the pages, quickly becoming immersed and sitting in the chair to read. There was so much to learn. Julia's body was going to do a lot of incredible things over the next six months. As would the baby. Apparently, she'd soon be able to feel the baby kick. *The baby.* It was still difficult to wrap his head around it, but it was getting a little easier with every passing minute, and a kick he could understand.

Julia seemed in a bit of a mood when she got out of the bathroom, but Logan knew the wedding weighed heavily on her mind, so he didn't bother saying anything, preferring instead to keep things light and upbeat. After he showered and dressed, they were off to the church by nine thirty. The ceremony was at eleven, to be followed by lunch and dancing until early evening, which suited Logan just fine. It meant more time for his night with Julia, the one where they finally set their future on the right path.

They ran into the woman from the bridal shop in the church parking lot.

"Everything go okay with the alterations?" Julia asked.

The woman nodded as she handed over a garment bag. "It did. There was enough fabric in the side seams to let it out. Good luck with the pregnancy."

Julia smiled, but Logan knew that particular grin, and it wasn't one she used when she was happy. It was for those moments when she had to fake it. "Uh-huh. Thank you."

The woman left while Logan and Julia walked inside.

"You okay?" he asked.

"Doesn't it seem weird that she mentioned the pregnancy out loud?"

Logan shrugged. "I guess. But isn't she the one who figured it out?"

Julia clutched the garment bag to her chest. "We asked the women in the shop not to say anything. Do you think somebody could've said something? I really don't want us to have to deal with the press again."

Logan hated seeing her so on edge, just as much as he hated the idea of battling the media again. He gripped her elbow and kissed her temple. "Don't be paranoid. It'll be fine."

"Okay." She didn't seem at all convinced. "I have to go get dressed. Then I need to check on the flowers one last time."

"Sounds like a plan. I have to do a few things for Carter, but I'll meet you in the chapel if I can."

"Okay." Her tone was annoyed, but she was worried about the notion of the press returning. Precisely the reason to wait for peace and calm to pop the question.

They parted, Logan finding the room where the groomsmen were camped out. "How's Tracy's future husband?" Logan asked Carter, who was in his tux and pacing, about to wear a path in the carpet.

Carter tugged at the collar. "I already hate this thing. And I can't stop sweating."

Logan clapped him on the shoulder. "Just sit and relax. You're going to do great today. It'll all be fine. I promise." Logan had apparently been put in charge of keeping everyone calm, a job he readily accepted today. For once, he felt as though he could see ahead, to the future. He had a clear course to take. A purpose. "I need to get dressed."

Logan ducked into a small adjacent room to put on his tux. He was putting in his cufflinks when Carter poked his head in. "Julia's out in the hall. She says she needs to talk to you right away. I think she's panicking again."

What now? Please don't let it be the press. "Okay. I'll be right out." He slipped into his jacket and rushed out into the hall.

She knocked the breath right out of him when he saw her. Sure, he'd seen her in the dress at the bridal shop, but this was different and not just because it actually fit her now. Her hair was up in an elegant twist; the morning light from the arched windows that lined the hall cast her in a heavenly glow. She was so gorgeous—so perfect. And his. Now he understood what Carter had been saying about waiting for the other shoe to drop. Logan was damn lucky and he knew it.

"We have a problem," she blurted.

"Just one?" He stepped next to her, inhaling her

sweet scent. "Then I'd say we're doing great. You look absolutely gorgeous, by the way."

"Don't be so dismissive."

"I could say the same thing about you. You didn't even acknowledge my compliment." He circled his arms around her waist, wanting her close.

She took a deep breath and forced a smile. "Thank you. Now come with me." She grasped his hand and marched them into the chapel. "Look. It's a complete disaster."

His eyes darted all over the room, searching for evidence of catastrophe. "What is?"

"The peonies. They aren't pale pink. They're pale purple. They're practically lavender." She forged ahead up the aisle, and Logan had to hustle to keep up. "See what I mean?" She pointed to an arrangement attached to the end of the pew as if it were the most repulsive thing she'd ever seen.

She wasn't wrong. They were clearly purple. And who really cared at this point? "Considering everything that has happened over the past few days, this is so unimportant. You did your best, and that's all anyone can ask. In the end, Tracy and Carter will be married, and that's what really matters."

"You don't think she'll freak out?"

"If she does, tell her to freak out at me. You've done so much to make her happy, and that includes keeping a secret that totally backfired on you."

"Please don't say I told you so."

"I won't. I think you know now that it was a bad idea to keep the pregnancy from your family."

She bowed her head. "I do. I messed up. I completely ruined that moment with my mom and there's no getting it back. I think that's my problem. I'm trying to keep any more moments from being ruined."

He put his arm around her and pulled her close. "It will all change when the baby arrives. Your mom will forget all of that. You'll have your moment with her then." All he could think about was the proposal later. He wanted that to be perfect, too. He understood exactly how she felt. "You know, I was reading your pregnancy book this morning while you were in the shower."

"You did?"

"I did. I read all about how big the baby is right now and about how big it's going to get. I read about when you'll be able to feel it kick. That's exciting stuff." *I hope I get to be there.* There was still part of him that knew Julia could panic. Or change her mind. Or say no. And her reaction to something as simple as the color of flowers wasn't doing much to assuage his worry.

She bit into her lower lip, her mouth quivering. "That's so sweet."

"Why are you crying?"

"Because I don't know what to think anymore, Logan, that's why. Two days ago you were all hot to get married and then the minute we start getting along, you drop it. All I can think is that you're just waiting and hoping..." A sob came out of her. "Hoping that the baby is yours."

He pulled her into a hug, holding her close, not

wanting to ever go. "Of course I hope that the baby is mine. How could I not hope that?"

Julia's body tensed in such an immediate way that he knew he'd messed up.

He stood back, holding on to her shoulders. The sadness in her eyes had become more profound. "That's probably not the right way to put it. In fact, I know it's not the right way to put it." He couldn't explain himself further. It would ruin his plans for tonight. Guests would be walking into the church any minute now. There was no time.

"No. It's okay. I know what you mean. And you're just being honest."

He breathed a huge sigh of relief. "Exactly."

"You're just saying what's really in your heart. Which is that you only want to be with me if the baby is yours. You've convinced yourself that's the only way this works."

No no no. "That's not what I'm saying. I haven't convinced myself of anything. I love you, Jules, I told you that."

"You told me that you will always love me. It's not the same. And I need you to love the baby, completely. That's the only way this works. Unconditional love. No questions asked."

Visions of Julia's legion of scummy boyfriends shuffled through his mind, the guys who always treated her so badly. Was he strong enough to love a child who was a product of one of those pairings? The pairings that had ripped his heart out, and hers for that matter, over and over again? He wanted to be

able to say that he would love the baby uncondition-
ally from his or her very first breath, but the truth
was that it might take some getting used to. Not much.
But possibly a little. He would get there. He knew he
would. But if he was being honest, there was a chance
it would take time. "Am I not allowed to have a single
doubt?" He took her hand and led her to the far side
of the rectory as guests began to file in.

She crossed her arms, the hurt and betrayal radiating off of her. He wasn't doing any better. How
had they ended up back at square one again? Neither
of them truly trusting that the other would do what
they said they were going to do? "No, Logan. You
aren't. You aren't allowed to have a single doubt. I
don't see any way that two people stay together for
the long haul without setting aside every last doubt
in their head."

A low grumble escaped Logan's throat. "Love isn't
a destination. It takes work. A lot of work. And you're
being so stubborn about this."

"I have no choice but to be exactly that, Logan.
I can't let you break my heart again. It nearly killed
me the first time."

Nearly killed me. "Then we work it out. Again."
He couldn't hide his irritation with all of this.

She shook her head, tears welling at the corners of
her eyes. "My original plan was the safest. You and
I make great friends. We make great lovers. I think
we'll make a good mom and dad, but I think those
are separate things now. I don't know that we'll make
a good husband and wife."

"What are you saying?"

She wrapped her arms around her waist, tears now rolling down her cheek.

"No. No. Jules, don't bail on me." It felt as if his stomach was diving for the floor. This was classic Julia—form an opinion and steamroller ahead, even when her take on things might not be based in reality.

"You know what, Logan? This is part of me correcting my past mistakes. You said you didn't want to be with me when I viewed you as a project. Well, this is me telling you that you're not a project. You don't want me to fix you, fine. I'm done fixing. You figure it out."

"Hoping that the baby will be mine isn't the most selfish thing in the world. It's human. I'm human."

She shook her head. "Do you have any idea how lonely I felt the day I found I was pregnant? That was supposed to be a purely happy day. But all I could do was wonder how I was going to make this work." Her hand went to her belly, cupping the tiny mound that was there. "This child needs love, Logan. Pure and simple. Doesn't matter what color his skin is or how tall she ends up being. In the end, this tiny human being growing inside me is going to need love. If I have to be the only person who gives it, I'll do that. Because I can't sit by and wonder if and when you're going to get with the program. I won't do it. It's one thing when it's my heart on the line, but I won't hurt this child."

"I'm not trying to hurt anyone. I'm just being honest."

Now the tears were really streaming down Julia's face, streaking her makeup and blanching her skin. "You questioned my stance on the paternity test, but this is the exact moment I feared. I knew that the minute I did and we got an answer you weren't going to like, that would be the end of Logan and Julia, forever. I wasn't ready to shut the door on us. But unfortunately, this just makes it feel like you do. I can't let you do it again, Logan. I have to be stronger than that."

"Jules. Come on. Let's just talk. I beg you."

"I can't stay. Not like this." With a swish of her dress, she was gone. Straight down the aisle and right out of his life.

I should've known. I should've known it was too good to be true. Things aren't perfect for Logan and he has to take off. Just like last time.

Julia raced down the hall to the room where her sister was getting ready. She stopped in the doorway, unable to step inside, although she wasn't sure why. Her mom was there, standing by Tracy's side.

"No tears." Tracy looked into the vanity mirror as she adjusted a clip in her hair. "There will be no tears on my wedding day."

"The mother of the bride is entitled to cry, honey. It's practically a tradition." Their mother pulled a tissue from her purse and blew her nose.

Julia stood frozen, sucking in deep breaths as inconspicuously as possible. And to think she'd been worried that flowers or cakes or of course, her pregnancy secret might ruin her sister's wedding. The reality was she was one unkind word away from collapsing into a pathetic pile of pink organza on the floor.

"Hey, Jules. I didn't see you there," Tracy said.

"Yep. Just got here." Julia's lip trembled, but she tried to ignore it.

"Everything good?" Tracy asked.

"Yes. Of course." Her sister would have her perfect day if it killed her. Which meant Julia had to keep her desire to blubber her eyes out to herself.

"Are you okay, darling? Your voice sounds funny. And why are you practically standing out in the hall? Come inside or Carter might try to sneak a peek at the bride."

Julia stepped into the room and closed the door behind her. "I'm fine. Just a little choked up, that's all. It's Tracy's big day and we've been waiting for it for so long. I'm so incredibly happy for her."

Tracy caught her sister's gaze in the reflection of the mirror. She jutted out her lower lip. "Now you're going to make me cry. That's the sweetest thing I think you've ever said to me. Come here." Tracy turned and reached for Julia and good God, Jules couldn't have kept it together if she'd been paid to do it. "I'm so sorry about my behavior over the last few days," Tracy said. "I know I've been hard on you and I'm sorry. Someday, you'll be in my place and you'll understand why I got so caught up in everything. I swear, it'll make you crazy."

In my place. Julia was convinced she would never, ever be in her sister's place. Ever. She wasn't capable of keeping a relationship together. Call it self-sabotage. Call it something else. She messed it up every time, and there was no sign of her changing this pattern any time soon. She and Logan had their breakthrough, the one they'd tried to reach for years. Then it all came tumbling down.

"I'm sorry I caused so many problems. It was never my intention," Julia said.

"I know you didn't do it on purpose. And you'll understand when you're a bride."

A single tear leaked from the corner of Julia's eye and she felt it about to happen— an avalanche of emotion was starting, trembling and quaking, threatening to crush her flimsy composure. "I'm not ever going to be a bride. I'm never going to get married. I'm going to die alone." The crying started. She'd cried more in the last month than she cared to admit. It wasn't a good thing to feel so on edge all the time.

"Don't say that."

"It's true. I get involved with the wrong guys over and over again. I can't help myself."

"Did something happen with Logan? I thought you two were working things out."

"We were, but then he had to go and say something that made me realize he doesn't really love me the way I need him to love me."

"What happened?"

Julia got very quiet, realizing there was a lot more

to this explanation than simply recounting what happened. "The thing is, about the baby, I'm not sure if it's his. It might be the boyfriend I had briefly before him."

"Oh no." Her mother closed her eyes and scratched her temple.

"Please don't freak out. I'm sorry I'm dumping all of this on you right now. We have to walk into that church in a few minutes and everything. I just... I thought he and I had worked it out and that he'd come to terms with the possibility that the baby isn't his, but he clearly still has doubts."

"Well, of course he has doubts. It's okay to have doubts," Tracy said, grabbing a nail file from the vanity and shaping one of her nails. "Carter had all kinds of doubts when we got back together. About whether or not it would work. He was gun-shy, to say the least. I was the one who'd broken up with him, and I think he was afraid I was going to break his heart again."

Many of Logan's words echoed in Julia's head... everything he'd said about the ways in which he'd been sure Julia would break his heart. "But you worked through all of it. You're getting married. Everything is perfect now."

"Everything is not perfect. We worked through enough to say that taking a chance on each other is a good idea. It doesn't mean we don't still have doubts. That's just part of being a couple. If you sit around waiting for the moment when everything is perfect, you're going to miss out on a lot."

Julia couldn't believe what was coming out of

Tracy's mouth. "But Logan said that even though he loves me, he's still nervous about how he'll feel if the baby isn't his. And he was dead-set on getting married two days ago. Now that it's a little more real, he hasn't said a word about that. Doesn't that seem like an awfully damning detail?"

Their mother stepped forward and shook her head. "Jules, do you have any idea what you're asking of him? It takes a big man to accept another man's responsibility, if that's the way this ends up. Of course he's going to have doubts. He's a first-time dad. Being a parent means you doubt everything and most of it comes down to worry that you won't measure up. Look at the relationship he had with his own dad. I'm sure he's worried about filling those shoes. It's not necessarily a reflection of you or the way he feels about you. Logan is a good man with a big heart, and he's wanted to be with you for more than twelve years. I think it's time you finally gave him the benefit of the doubt."

Julia's stomach sank. "So you're saying I messed up. Again."

"Yes. Yes, I am."

Nothing like being real, Mom.

"The good thing about mistakes is they can almost always be fixed."

A knock came at the door. "Five minutes until we're ready for the bride."

"Are you going to be okay, Jules?" Tracy asked.

Once again, totally not okay. Julia composed herself, glancing in the mirror and wiping away a smudge of mascara with her pinkie. "Yes. I'm great. My sister is getting married. That's all I really care about right now."

Fourteen

The ceremony was torture. Standing up there, feet away from Logan, all while the room was filled with the heady scent of flowers and the knowledge that everyone in attendance was witnessing true love. Julia knew they were, and she was happy for her sister, but it only underscored one fact—this was one place she would never be.

When it came to the vows, Julia did everything she could to keep it together, but it was nearly impossible. The gasps and cries coming out of her mother in the front row weren't helping. Then there was Logan. She watched as he listened intently. The man had enough good looks for seven men, but that wasn't what she loved about him. She loved him for his persistence with her; she loved him for the ways he pushed for what he wanted. She loved him for his heart, which she knew from experience was the best place to ever be.

How could one person be everything she ever wanted and still feel impossible to hold on to? Where was the fairness in that? Nowhere, that's where. But did it really matter? She might not have pushed him away the last time, but she'd pushed him away today, just as she'd pushed him away before. The pushing had to stop. The insecurities inside her, the ones that said she would never be good enough for him, were just going to have to learn to shut up. She had to make things right. She had to find a way to claim her one millionth chance to turn things around.

When it came time to walk down the aisle with him, she didn't waste a second. "We have to talk," she muttered out of the side of her mouth, with a big smile plastered to her face.

Logan smiled, too, but she knew it was for show, not his reaction to her. "Tell me about it."

They stood in the receiving line for a good half hour, shaking hands, kissing cheeks. Then it was time to go in to the reception. Every time Julia thought she'd catch a stray minute, someone would come up to her and start talking. Or they would drag Logan off to chat with someone else. It was a nightmare—no privacy, no alone time, no chance to just talk this out.

When it came time for toasts, she operated on autopilot. She read it exactly as she'd written it, not nearly as well as Logan, the man with the wonderful way with words. All she could think about was being on the beach a mere twenty-four hours ago, the world falling apart and coming together all at the same time. Her entire existence changed with Logan. It was different. It was better. And she was desperate to get back there. Again. Her mother and sister were right. It was horrible of her to hold Logan to such unrealistic standards.

"Let's all raise a glass to Tracy and Carter," she said, lifting her champagne glass, which was full of ginger ale. The bubbles tickled her nose; tears tickled her eyes. The room was so full of love it nearly made her sick. Would Logan accept hers? What reason did he have aside from the baby? It would be easier on him if he just walked away. There was no doubt in her mind about that.

Logan clinked his fork against the side of his glass and stood. His focus was on Tracy and Carter, exactly as it should have been, but she longed for even a glance, a single flicker of his warm eyes. One look that would tell her that everything would be okay. That he would forgive her. "Just as Julia spoke of fate, I had originally planned to talk about the same thing today. And why wouldn't I? We all look at Tracy and Carter and know that they're meant to be together. It feels like fate that they found each other. Julia said exactly that." His normally strong voice wobbled, and he cleared his throat. "But what I want to talk about and toast to is perfection, or more specifically, the need to cast aside the notion of finding the perfect person. Because the truth is that Carter and Tracy aren't perfect. Neither one of them."

Carter shrugged and slugged back the last of the champagne in his glass, which brought a laugh from the guests and a welcome moment of levity.

"But together, as a couple, Carter and Tracy are perfect. They are there for each other. They don't let each other down. And when they do, they know how to say they're sorry."

Julia's breaths had grown so shallow she thought they might evaporate. Was this Logan's way of telling her that she'd done exactly that? She'd let him down. She would own up to it. She would say she was sorry. If he gave her the chance.

"They know how to forgive and ask for forgiveness," he continued. "They know to hold on to each other and not let go, because that is more important than anything."

With that, Logan looked at Julia intently, their gazes connecting, sending a steeplechase of goose bumps over her skin. His expression was difficult to read though and that filled her with familiar doubt. She wanted to think that she saw openness in his incredible eyes. She wanted to believe he would listen to her one more time, and that he wasn't instead holding her up as an example of the ways people don't manage to hold on to each other.

Logan turned his sights to the room of family and friends before them. "I'm not perfect," Logan continued. "I have made every mistake in the book. I have fallen short and I have failed. I've failed some of the most important people in my life. I'm not perfect. We're all imperfect." He glanced over at Julia again, this time looking much more deeply into her eyes. She was hanging on every word, still finding it nearly impossible to breathe. "But the beautiful thing about life is that if you find another person to love, your imperfections aren't important. Two imperfect people can make a perfect pair." He pressed his lips together and looked away. "With that, I want to wish Tracy and Carter a long and happy life together."

Logan sat down after his toast, hoping like hell that had done the trick. What else could he do? If Julia had decided that whatever he had to offer simply wasn't enough, there wasn't much to be done. How many times could he plead his case? It was nearly impossible to convince her of anything, but at least he could say that he'd made a strong argument.

The DJ made an announcement that it was time for Carter and Tracy's first dance. He watched as they made their way out to the dance floor, Tracy in her elegant white gown and Carter in his charcoal-gray tux. They seemed as happy as two people could be. *I want what they have.* His plan to get one step closer to his own wedding now seemed stupid. He should have given Julia the ring yesterday, when she was happy. He should have remembered just how tenuous things were between them and been more mindful of that.

Carter and Tracy started their dance, staring into each other's eyes, and gracefully swaying back and forth in each other's arms.

Julia, however, was playing musical chairs. She slid into the seat her sister had been occupying minutes ago, one seat closer to him. She patted the empty chair that had been Carter's. "Come here," she whispered.

He nearly asked if this was a trick, but he couldn't deny his natural inclination to want to be closer to her. He obliged. "Yes?"

"I wasn't kidding when I said that we need to talk."

"Okay. When?"

"Now?"

"The bride and groom are having their first dance. Don't you think we should stay to see that?"

She looked out at the dance floor and bobbed her head three times. "Okay. We saw it. Time to talk."

He laughed quietly. "For someone who was so concerned with making her sister happy, you don't seem to care much about it now."

She grasped his arm and squeezed, hard. "I'm more concerned with making us happy."

His breath caught in his throat. Maybe his speech really had worked. "Okay. Where?"

"Come with me." She took his hand and they made a careful and quiet exit, going out through the side of the reception hall, outside, and up a set of stairs to a wide stone balcony with a view of the Cape Fear River running alongside the downtown river walk.

When she stopped, she turned to him and took both hands, squinting into the sun. "I'm an idiot. I'm a total dummy and you're just going to have to find a way to forgive me. Let's get a paternity test right away. I'll do anything I can to have a shot at keeping you for real. We'll put all of it to rest and I'll have to trust that fate will keep us together somehow. We'll just do it. Rip it off like a Band-Aid."

If only she knew the thoughts that had run through his head during the ceremony, about the things he'd said. "We don't have to rely on fate, Jules. I don't want a paternity test. Frankly, you're as much of a test as I can handle."

She smiled softly. "Funny. I could say the same thing about you."

"Believe me, I know." He looked down at his feet, then out at the water, searching for the right words to say. Thoughts of Julia, of the baby, and of his dad had been cycling through his head all day. "I've spent an awful lot of my life hoping to live up to what my dad had wanted for me, the accolades and awards. Trying like hell to win a World Series. But after talking to your father last night, I really realized how much my dad loved his kids. He didn't catch a million pitches for me because he loved baseball. He did it because he loved me. This child deserves the same, and I know I'm capable of giving it. I'm not going to pass up the chance to do that. I don't need a test to prove to myself that I can."

"It's okay to have your reservations. I can live with them. I was being unreasonable and expecting you to conform to everything I wanted. I can trust that it will all work out." She smiled up at him, her face so eager and hopeful. "I can trust that we will work out."

"You don't have to worry about my reservations. There aren't any anymore. The last few hours, thinking about losing you again, all I could think was that I didn't doubt for a second that I wanted this. I wanted us, with the baby. The only hitch is that I need to know that you're on board. I need to know that you're in it for the long haul."

She blew out a breath and her eyes lit up, even out there in the bright sun. "I'm more than in it. I'm so sorry about this morning. I freaked out because it took me right back to that place where I was terrified of seeing you walk away."

He nodded, taking in every word, everything he'd wanted to hear from her. There was no way he was waiting another minute to start their future together. It had to start now. "Before I ask you what I need to ask you, I need to say one thing. No more talk of a paternity test. It's a dead issue."

"Okay…" A quizzical look crossed her face. "I know that's been difficult for you."

Here goes nothing. And everything. He dropped down to his knee, holding her hand.

Her other hand flew to her lips. "No."

"You're saying no already?"

Her head nearly rattled back and forth. "Not what I mean. I'm sorry. Go ahead."

He snickered. "Julia Keys, will you marry me? Will you be my wife? Will you parent with me and live happily ever after with me?"

She nodded, but a word didn't come out of her mouth.

"Marry me and have our baby. Nobody needs to think anything else. I don't care if the baby looks like me. Hell, if we're lucky, the baby will just look like you." He reached into his pocket for his grandmother's ring, something he'd thought about hundreds of times since his mother had given it to him. He slid it out of the pouch and held it up for her.

"Where did you get that?"

"It was my grandmother's. My dad's mom. My mother gave it to me the other day when we were over at the house."

"You've had it all this time?"

"You know, when you first told me that you were pregnant, and I insisted that we get married, that was my way of being a man and taking care of things. That was my way of trying to be a dad. And given that I was only a few minutes into it, I realize now that I wasn't doing that great of a job."

"What does that have to do with the ring?"

"I'm trying to say that I don't give this ring lightly. I've never even thought of putting it on another woman's finger. I think it's because I knew all along that I was waiting for you. I'm dying to put it on your finger. I'm dying to hear you say that you'll be my wife and we can have the happily-ever-after that we've spent more than a dozen years waiting on."

"I love you so much, Logan. Of course I'll marry you."

He stood and slipped the ring onto her finger. It didn't quite fit. "I'm sorry. It's a little tight."

"Bloating." She crammed the ring the rest of the way on to her hand. "Normal pregnancy stuff."

He leaned over and kissed her. "You make it sound so sexy."

She rested her forehead against his and they fell into a snug embrace. "I'm worried about one thing, though."

"No. No worrying. We're done worrying. I don't care if the forecast is for hail and the sky is going to fall. No more worrying."

She bugged her eyes at him. "I was just wondering whether it's rude to get engaged at someone else's wedding."

"Considering all of the very rude things that have happened at our hand over the last few days, an engagement is the least of our worries. We'll just have to keep it our little secret."

"Oh, because we all know how good we are at doing that."

"This one is different. We're both fully invested in it."

"What about the actual wedding? We should probably talk about that at some point."

Good thing he'd thought about this yesterday during the rehearsal. "Yeah, about that. I guess we should do it here in town. For our parents?"

"Yes. Perfect. How about Monday morning?"

"Monday? But that's the day after tomorrow. There's no time to plan. We have to get the license and you'll have to find a dress. And then we'll have to find someone to officiate."

She shook her head and planted her hands on her hips. "If only we knew a judge…"

"My mom."

"Yes. I don't want to go through what Tracy just

went through. I just want to get to the good part. Being with you."

He pulled her against him and gave her another kiss, soft and steamy. "You are so brilliant. I can't wait to get you back to the hotel."

She grabbed his wrist and consulted his watch. "Cake gets cut in fifteen minutes. Everyone should be hammered by a half hour after that. I say we make our escape then." Still holding his arm, she turned to head for the stairs, attempting to pull him along.

"Hey, Jules?" He tugged her back.

"Yes?"

"I think you were right. I should write a memoir."

She smiled the most beautiful smile he'd ever seen, which was saying a lot. "What changed your mind?"

"Now I know it's going to have a happy ending."

Epilogue

Julia stopped in her tracks in the hall outside the master bedroom of Logan's Connecticut estate—*their* estate, now that they had been husband and wife for five and a half crazy, but ridiculously happy, months. She slapped her hands against the wall, pushing her hands into the plaster. The pain was unlike anything she'd experienced, a relentless tightening starting in her back and coiling around her midsection. It left her restless, with a desire to do conflicting things—sit and stand, move and freeze, stay silent and scream.

As she'd learned to do in childbirth class, she tried to visualize anything that felt good. Right now, mental images of their dreamy honeymoon in French Polynesia were the only thing getting her through the contractions. She and Logan had spent two weeks in a thatched-roof villa several hundred yards offshore, on stilts above the clear, emerald-green sea. Their days were filled with exquisite food, skinny-dips in their private pool, lovemaking and a nap every afternoon. At night after dinner, they climbed into the hammock and spent hours talking, snug in each other's arms, warmed by soft ocean breezes, body heat and the deep satisfaction that came with knowing they belonged together. They'd made it. And it was perfect.

"You've got this. A few more seconds." Logan continued to apply counterpressure on her lower back with his hand.

As if his words were magic, the tightening released her and she could move again. "Oh, thank God."

He consulted the stopwatch on his phone. "Still eight minutes apart. About forty-five seconds per contraction. Do you want me to call the hospital again? I feel like this isn't moving very quickly."

"They told us it can take a really long time the first time. I don't want to end up in a hospital bed for hours on end. I'd rather be here with you."

He sweetly brushed her hair away from her face. "I know, hon. I just want to make sure you and the baby are safe and healthy." Approaching from the side to avoid her impressive belly, he wrapped his arms around her shoulders and kissed her temple.

She smiled and took his hand. "And I love you for it. Let's just keep walking and we'll call after a few more contractions."

"Sounds like a deal. Which way are we headed?"

"Kitchen. I need food."

The trip downstairs was slow and deliberate, Logan's arm around her as she gripped the ornate wrought iron banister. She loved this house—it was grand, but homey, and they had all sorts of privacy. She loved being permanently on the same coast as her parents, Logan's mom, and Tracy and Carter. It would be a quick trip for the grandparents to fly up to dote on their grandchild. If Tracy and Carter decided to have a baby, it would give them more chances to get the cousins together.

Julia toddled from the bottom of the stairs into the kitchen, her belly leading the way. "I just want something simple. Orange juice and an English muffin."

"Good, since that's the extent of my culinary skills." Logan went to work while Julia perched on the edge of a bar stool at the kitchen island, surveying the view through the stretch of multiple French doors overlooking the grounds behind the house. Early March and snow was still on the ground, something she was getting used to. She usually spent this time of year at her beach house in Malibu, just to stay away from the cold. "We need to call about having the pool fence put in as soon as the snow has melted. Otherwise, time will get away from us and the next thing we know, the baby will be walking and we'll both be worried sick about him or her getting outside and falling in."

"I already called this morning. After your first few contractions. I figure we'll have our hands full in the next few weeks. I didn't want to risk forgetting."

"Good thinking."

"That's why you love me." He handed her a glass of juice and smiled that electric Logan smile.

"That's part of it." She grinned back at him. There were days with Logan when she was tempted to wonder if this was all a dream. It was about far more than ending up with the charming, ridiculously handsome athlete. He was her best friend. They made each other whole. She'd spent a dozen years convinced they'd never get on the same page at the same time. But this certainly wasn't a dream—it was better. They hadn't been handed this on a silver platter. She and Logan had worked hard for their life together.

The toaster popped, and Logan buttered the English muffin, bringing it to her on a small plate. Ravenous, Julia took a huge bite, but that was all she got before her body decided to take over. She leaned against the kitchen counter, bracing herself, dropping her head and breathing through the pain.

Logan was quickly at her side again. "Do you want me to rub your back?"

She shook her head vigorously, the pain nearly impossible to take. "Honestly? Don't. Touch. Me."

He took a step back as if she were a bomb about to go off. "Are they getting more intense?"

She couldn't speak. She nodded.

"I think we should go to the hospital."

Finally, her muscles began to uncoil. Her shoulders dropped in relief, and she caught her breath as warmth rippled down her upper thighs. She wondered for a moment if it was just being around Logan. He did have that effect on her, but as much as she loved him, she was feeling anything but romantic right now. The heat trailed down her leg. Liquid trickled onto the polished wood floor. She stared down as the pool of fluid grew. "Oh my God. My water broke."

"Your hospital bag is already in the car. I'll get your coat. And a towel."

He's so calm and collected in a crisis. "No coat. I'm a human furnace right now. And I'd get two towels if I were you."

"One minute."

He flew up the stairs and she soon heard the slamming of cabinet doors. He was back and ready to go before she could finish her English muffin. Frenetic energy radiated from him as he nervously nodded his head and helped her up from her seat. He was ready to go. He was ready for this to happen. She was ready, too. She was tired of feeling like a human beluga.

Rushing to the hospital ushered in a chaotic mix of excitement, anticipation and worry. Logan felt too much as if everything was happening *to* them and not because of them. They certainly had no control over the things Julia's body was doing, the immense pain she was having to endure. She suffered through the car ride, but remained quiet and focused. He admired her strength, but was not surprised by her determination to make it seem as if she had everything under control.

Now that he was putting their new minivan through its paces, navigating S-turns and tight corners, Logan was happy to learn just how well it handled. He'd never expected he'd own a car like this, nor did he expect that being behind the wheel of this car would make him feel more like a man than any of the expensive sports cars he owned. It made him feel like a dad.

He got them there in record time and zipped into a parking spot near the emergency entrance. An orderly dashed outside to help Julia into a wheelchair and get her inside. Logan juggled a clipboard a nurse had handed him, along with his phone and Julia's bag. He fielded questions about contractions and Julia's due date as she was wheeled into an exam room.

It didn't take hospital staff long to get her into a gown and up on the exam table. A doctor checked her, then rolled back on a stool and scribbled on Julia's chart. "She's nearly five centimeters. You're lucky you didn't stay at home much longer. You might've been having your baby in the car. Let's get you admitted and up into Labor and Delivery."

Julia's sweet eyes flashed up at Logan. They were filled with both optimism and fear. She seemed to be feeling much as he did—like they were riding a corkscrew roller coaster on Christmas morning.

He leaned down and kissed her forehead. "You're doing such a good job. I'm so proud of you."

"Thanks. I'm nervous."

Yes, darling. Me, too.

They were quickly registered and taken to a Labor and Delivery room. The nurses were a godsend— calm and capable through countless unfamiliar experiences: monitors that beeped, cords that lit up, and a constant parade of people in and out of the room. Julia got something to take the edge off the pain, but it was still very much there, and Logan would've done anything to take it all away from her.

She endured the contractions for hours. Logan did his part, talking her through it, reminding her to breathe, holding a cool washcloth to her forehead and giving her ice chips. Still, he felt so helpless that it had turned into a test of his mental endurance. How long can you watch the person you love most in the world suffer? He was desperate to make this easier for her and there was absolutely nothing he could do.

After nearly six hours, they were both exhausted, but Julia was showing the greatest effects of it. Her face was red and puffy, her eyes tired. They'd been left alone for at least the last forty-five minutes, and he was really starting to worry. Why wasn't anyone helping them? Why wasn't the baby here yet? He was just about to call someone when a nurse they hadn't yet met barged through the door.

"I think you're ready to push, Mom." The nurse bunched up the sleeves of the shirt she was wearing under scrubs and washed her hands. "Baby should be here very soon."

"Um, okay," Julia said, seeming as confused as Logan felt.

"I'm sorry. Who are you?" he asked.

"I'm Maria. I just came on shift about twenty minutes ago." She snapped on a pair of latex gloves. "I've been watching your contractions on the monitor. I think you're ready."

How someone could know it was time for the baby to arrive merely by looking on a television monitor was beyond Logan, but he was in no position to argue. "Okay. What can I do?"

"Help me get her feet in the stirrups."

Logan did as he was asked while Julia moaned with the pain of another contraction.

Maria did the quick examination. "Ten centimeters. Fully dilated. I can see the top of the baby's head, if you want to look, Dad."

Logan was struggling to keep up—holding Julia's hand, wanting to see the baby while also being scared to see the baby. The only logical question sprang from his lips. "The doctor?"

"Should be here any minute. But don't worry. I've caught lots of babies." She blew her curly black hair from her forehead and winked at Logan. "Another contraction, Mom?"

Julia nodded and scrunched up her face.

"Dad, help her sit up to push."

Logan took Julia's arm and again did as he was told.

"Bear down. Push as hard as you can. That's great. You can do it." Maria was a font of encouragement.

"Childbearing hips, my ass," Julia grunted, followed by a low and agonizing groan. When the final sound passed her lips, she collapsed back on the bed and turned to Logan. "Even though I love you, I hate you."

He smiled wide. "So nothing has changed."

"Very funny."

He leaned down and pressed a kiss to her forehead, which was damp with perspiration. "I love you more than you'll ever know."

"The baby is crowning. I think only one or two more pushes like that last one. Looks like he or she has a pretty impressive head of dark hair.'"

"That's a good sign," Julia muttered.

Indeed, it was, although Logan would've taken a bald baby or a baby with clown hair at this point. He just wanted the little bugger to get here.

Julia pushed like a champ through two more contractions. "I don't want to stop. I can't not push."

"That's good. Just keep going. The baby is almost here," Maria said.

Logan didn't bother to bring up the fact that the doctor hadn't arrived. Maria had more than convinced him she knew what she was doing.

"Here comes the head. One more push and you're home free." Maria stood and kicked the stool out from under her.

Julia folded herself in half, her face turning nearly purple, not a sound coming from her. Instead, a squishing noise came from the end of the bed. Followed by a cry.

"It's a girl," Maria exclaimed, pure joy in her voice.

Another nurse walked in and saw what was happening. She rushed to help Maria clean up the baby and swaddle her.

Logan turned to Julia. Tears were running right

down her face, but she was smiling ear to ear. He was in a similar state—consumed by happiness and relief. "A girl. It's a girl."

"I know. Oh my God. It's so amazing. I want to see her." Julia was still catching her breath.

"It'll be just a minute," Maria answered as the baby continued to cry. "Then we'll get her to you."

"You're going to be stuck in a house with two women," Julia said. "How's that going to work for the guy who grew up with only brothers?"

He leaned down and kissed her cheek at least a dozen times, wiping away her tears with his lips. "I think it sounds wonderful."

"Here's Baby Girl Brandt," Maria said, presenting Julia with a tiny bundle of baby tightly wrapped in a striped flannel blanket. "I'll leave you three some time to get acquainted. She's perfect. Congratulations."

Julia held the baby looking like she was born to do this. "Sophie?"

He nodded. "After my grandmother."

"The original owner of my ring."

He reached out and rubbed Sophie's cheek with the back of his hand. Her skin was a bit purple and splotchy, but tender and new. Her lips were sweet and pink and she had the most adorable tiny nose. She was incredibly quiet, eyes wide open and alert. "She's beautiful. Just like her mom." Logan couldn't even comprehend how lucky he was. It was unfathomable. He only knew that he was blessed.

Julia peeked under Sophie's hat. "Looks like some serious curly hair under there."

Logan leaned closer and looked. "So she does."

"A little bit like you had when you were younger."

Logan didn't need to weigh in on it. There was so much better left unsaid. They were a family. And a happy one at that.

* * * * *

Pick up all the flirty and fun
Harlequin Desire novels from
Karen Booth

THAT NIGHT WITH THE CEO
PREGNANT BY THE RIVAL CEO
THE CEO DADDY NEXT DOOR

Available now!

If you're on Twitter, tell us what you think
of Harlequin Desire! #harlequindesire

REQUEST YOUR FREE BOOKS!
2 FREE NOVELS PLUS 2 FREE GIFTS!

HARLEQUIN®

Desire

ALWAYS POWERFUL, PASSIONATE AND PROVOCATIVE

YES! Please send me 2 FREE Harlequin® Desire novels and my 2 FREE gifts (gifts are worth about $10). After receiving them, if I don't wish to receive any more books, I can return the shipping statement marked "cancel." If I don't cancel, I will receive 6 brand-new novels every month and be billed just $4.55 per book in the U.S. or $5.24 per book in Canada. That's a savings of at least 13% off the cover price! It's quite a bargain! Shipping and handling is just 50¢ per book in the U.S. and 75¢ per book in Canada.* I understand that accepting the 2 free books and gifts places me under no obligation to buy anything. I can always return a shipment and cancel at any time. Even if I never buy another book, the two free books and gifts are mine to keep forever.

225/326 HDN GH2P

Name _____ (PLEASE PRINT) _____

Address _____ Apt. # _____

City _____ State/Prov. _____ Zip/Postal Code _____

Signature (if under 18, a parent or guardian must sign) _____

Mail to the **Reader Service:**
IN U.S.A.: P.O. Box 1867, Buffalo, NY 14240-1867
IN CANADA: P.O. Box 609, Fort Erie, Ontario L2A 5X3

Want to try two free books from another line?
Call 1-800-873-8635 or visit www.ReaderService.com.

* Terms and prices subject to change without notice. Prices do not include applicable taxes. Sales tax applicable in N.Y. Canadian residents will be charged applicable taxes. Offer not valid in Quebec. This offer is limited to one order per household. Not valid for current subscribers to Harlequin Desire books. All orders subject to credit approval. Credit or debit balances in a customer's account(s) may be offset by any other outstanding balance owed by or to the customer. Please allow 4 to 6 weeks for delivery. Offer available while quantities last.

Your Privacy—The Reader Service is committed to protecting your privacy. Our Privacy Policy is available online at www.ReaderService.com or upon request from the Reader Service.

We make a portion of our mailing list available to reputable third parties that offer products we believe may interest you. If you prefer that we not exchange your name with third parties, or if you wish to clarify or modify your communication preferences, please visit us at www.ReaderService.com/consumerchoice or write to us at Reader Service Preference Service, P.O. Box 9062, Buffalo, NY 14240-9062. Include your complete name and address.

HDI5

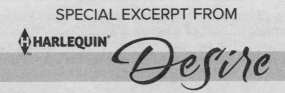
*A billionaire investigator and his assistant vow to bring
down a crime family even as they protect an orphaned
baby from the fallout—and give in to their undeniable
attraction! But the secrets she's keeping may destroy all
they've been working for...*

Read on for a sneak peek at
THE HEIR'S UNEXPECTED BABY
by Jules Bennett, part of the bestselling
***BILLIONAIRES AND BABIES** series!*

"What are you doing here so early?"

Jack Carson brushed past Vivianna Smith and stepped
into her apartment, trying like hell not to touch her. Or
breathe in that familiar jasmine scent. Or think of how sexy
she looked in that pale pink suit.

Masochist. That's all he could chalk this up to. But he
had a mission, damn it, and he needed his assistant's help
to pull it off.

"I need you to use that charm of yours and get more
information about the O'Sheas." He turned to face her as
she closed the door.

The O'Sheas might run a polished high-society auction
house, but he knew they were no better than common
criminals. And Jack was about to bring them down in a
spectacular show of justice. His ticket was the woman who
fueled his every fantasy.

Vivianna moved around him to head down the hall to the
nursery. "I'm on your side here," she told him with a soft

smile. "Why don't you come back this evening and I'll make dinner and we can figure out our next step."

Dinner? With her and the baby? That all sounded so… domestic. He prided himself on keeping work in the office or in neutral territory. But he'd come here this morning to check on her…and he couldn't blame it all on the O'Sheas.

Damn it.

"You can come to my place and I'll have my chef prepare something." There. If Tilly was on hand, then maybe it wouldn't seem so family-like. "Any requests?" he asked.

Did her gaze just dart to his lips? She couldn't look at him with those dark eyes as if she wanted…

No. It didn't matter what she wanted, or what he wanted for that matter. Their relationship was business only.

Jack paused, soaking in the sight of her in that prim little suit, holding the baby. Definitely time to go before he forgot she actually worked for him and took what he'd wanted for months…

Don't miss
THE HEIR'S UNEXPECTED BABY
by Jules Bennett,
available February 2017 wherever
Harlequin® Desire books and ebooks are sold.

If you enjoyed this excerpt, pick up a new
BILLIONAIRES AND BABIES *book every month!*

It's the #1 bestselling series from Harlequin® Desire—
Powerful men…wrapped around their babies' little
fingers.

www.Harlequin.com

Whatever You're Into... Passionate Reads

Looking for more passionate reads from Harlequin®?
Fear not! Harlequin® Presents, Harlequin® Desire and
Harlequin® Blaze offer you irresistible romance stories
featuring powerful heroes.

❦ HARLEQUIN® *Presents*®

Do you want alpha males, decadent glamour and jet-set
lifestyles? Step into the sensational, sophisticated world of
Harlequin® Presents, where sinfully tempting heroes ignite a
fierce and wickedly irresistible passion!

❦ HARLEQUIN® *Desire*

Harlequin® Desire novels are powerful, passionate and
provocative contemporary romances set against a backdrop of
wealth, privilege and sweeping family saga. Alpha heroes with
a soft side meet strong willed but vulnerable heroines amid a
dramatic world of divided loyalties, high-stakes conflict and
intense emotion.

❦ HARLEQUIN® *Blaze*

Harlequin® Blaze stories sizzle with strong heroines and
irresistible heroes playing the game of modern love and lust.
They're fun, sexy and always steamy.

Be sure to check out our full selection of books
within each series every month!

www.Harlequin.com

HPASSION2016